D0857600

THE
MOONSHINE
WAR

Elmore Leonard

THE MOONSHINE WAR

WHEELER
PUBLISHING, INC.
ROCKLAND, MA

★ AN AMERICAN COMPANY ★

Published in Large Print by arrangement with The Doubleday Broadway Publishing Group, a division of Random House, Inc., in the United States and Canada.

Wheeler Large Print Book Series.

Set in 16 pt Plantin.

Library of Congress Cataloging-in-Publication Data

Leonard, Elmore, 1925-
    The moonshine war / Elmore Leonard.
        p. (large print) cm.(Wheeler large print book series)
    ISBN 1-58724-106-4 (hardcover)
    1. Prohibition—Fiction. 2. Distilling, Illicit—Fiction. 3. Large type books. I. Title. II. Series

[PS3562.E55 M66 2001]
813'.54—dc21   2001046591
                                                    CIP

For
JIM BILL SIMPSON *and* BUCK BESHEAR

one

The war began the first Saturday in June 1931, when Mr. Baylor sent a boy up to Son Martin's place to tell him they were coming to raid his still.

The boy was sixteen and had lived in the mountains all his life, but at first he wasn't sure he wanted to go up there alone. He asked Mr. Baylor how he was supposed to get there, and Mr. Baylor said they'd lend him an official Sheriff's Department Ford car. He told Mr. Baylor he had only seen this man Son Martin about twice before, since the man hardly ever showed himself; maybe he'd go up there and tell the wrong person. Mr. Baylor, who was seventy-three years old and sheriff of the county, said to the boy, well, if you go up there and knock on his door and the man answers it is a white man that's Son Martin. If it's a nigger opens it, that's Aaron, his hired man. Mr. Baylor said, now if you can tell a white man from a nigger you're all set, aren't you?

The boy said, yes, sir, he'd do it; but he asked Mr. Baylor, if they were going to raid the man's still, why was the man being told about it? And Mr. Baylor said, don't worry about that, just tell him.

1

The boy's name was Lowell Holbrook, Jr. Evenings he wore a white jacket over his big bony shoulders and worked at the Hotel Cumberland as a bellboy, taking the grips and sample cases from the Louisville salesmen and lugging them upstairs. The few times he had seen Son Martin had been in the hotel: the man standing at the desk with his hat on the counter, leaning against it and talking to Mrs. Lyons, the manager. Son Martin was a good friend of Mrs. Lyons; everybody knew that. Some boys said they were more than good friends, that they were going to bed together, but Lowell couldn't picture Mrs. Lyons doing that.

Afternoons Lowell fooled around somewhere, maybe over at the Feed & Seed store, or hung around the courthouse if he wanted to make any extra money. The county people were always sending papers to somebody to have signed and wanting something picked up. They knew Lowell was fast and reliable because he worked at the hotel, and he had run errands for Mr. Baylor a lot of times before. Once he had driven all the way over to Corbin to pick up an important document. He had also been up by Broke-Leg Creek plenty of times and knew the road to Son Martin's place. But he had never been near the house. Some boys had told him, Son catches you on his land he'll blow your head off before asking your name. Lowell didn't think about it backing out of the parking space by the courthouse or driving through town.

The Saturday afternoon traffic kept him busy: the mud-washed cars and old trucks and mule wagons creeping along, the people gawking at the store windows and waving to friends. Nobody had enough money to spend more than a dollar; but, like most Saturdays lately, it was Cow Day and a person could buy a raffle ticket from any of the local merchants and maybe win himself a cow.

Lowell was hoping some of his buddies would see him driving the Sheriff's Department Ford car. Once out of town though, following the blacktop east for seven miles before turning off on a secondary road that climbed up into the scrub, Lowell began thinking about arriving at Son Martin's place and getting out of the car. There wasn't anything to be nervous about; Mr. Baylor wouldn't have sent him if there was. But he kept licking his lips anyway and wiping the back of his hand across his mouth. He said in his mind, Mr. Martin, I'm supposed to tell you they're coming up here to raid your whiskey still this evening. Jesus, then what does he say?

All the way up through the hollow the road was narrow and muddy and deep-rutted from the spring rains. It was hard enough staying in the tracks. Then the two foxhounds came bounding and barking out of the thicket, running next to the car and in front of it, so close sometimes Lowell couldn't see them. All he'd have to do was run over one of Son Martin's hounds. Then which did he tell first, about the whiskey raid or the hound? If the

3

hounds would shut up he could hear himself think and study on how to drive this road without going off in the brush.

But the hounds chased Lowell for a mile and a half up through the hollow and didn't break loose until he had reached the clearing and there was the house: a two-story, gray-weathered affair set against the right-hand slope and leveled with stilts so that the porch, on the side of the house as Lowell approached, was as high as a man's head. Beyond the house across the open yard, were the barn and outbuildings and Son Martin's pickup truck over by a shed. Lowell didn't see anything that looked like a whiskey still; there was smoke rising above the house, but that would be from the cookstove. Beyond the cleared land and pasture, the hills were dark with scrub oak and laurel and climbed in hollows and ridges up to the clear afternoon sky. Lowell could just make out the roof of another house way up in the trees. High above were jaggedy-looking sandstone outcrops and several open places that looked like dry creek beds, wide rivers of mud, where the terrible flash floods of '27 had washed away crops and timber. Some of the trees had been hauled out and milled for lumber; but there were still plenty of uprooted hunks lying dead at the edge of the pasture.

Reaching the crest of the road, the hounds streaking ahead of him across the yard, Lowell was going so slow the engine started to lug and he had to shift into second quick. He missed

4

the gear as his foot slipped off the clutch pedal, and the car made an awful metal-grinding noise. Coasting into the yard, punching the shifter looking for second gear, and sounding like a kid just learning to drive, Lowell saw the man on the porch waiting for him, standing with his hands in his back pockets.

The man didn't come down off the porch; he waited for Lowell to get out of the car. Lowell slammed the door behind him. It didn't catch tight, damn-it, but he kept going anyway, around the front of the car to within about ten feet of the porch steps. That was close enough.

"I'm supposed to tell you they're coming to raid your still this evening."

Son Martin didn't take his hands from his back pockets or say anything for a minute. He was wearing a brown shirt that looked like an army shirt. In the daylight he looked younger than the times Lowell had seen him in the hotel; but he knew the man wasn't young at all and must be about thirty-five. It was his hair and his face that made him seem young: full head of hair cut short and clean-looking bony face darkened by the sun. He looked like a soldier, that was it; he still looked like one.

Son Martin turned a little as he said, "You hear?"

Lowell noticed the handle of the Smith & Wesson sticking out of Son's back pocket. Past him, Lowell could make out somebody standing inside the screen door. "I guess it our turn," the man inside answered. The hired man, Aaron.

Son Martin was looking at Lowell again. "Who sent you?"

"Mr. Baylor did." Lowell snapped the answer back.

"In his office, that's where you talked to him?"

"Yes, sir."

Behind the screen Aaron said, "Ask him was anybody else there."

"Wasn't anybody," the boy said. "Just me and Mr. Baylor."

"You work at the hotel," Son Martin said.

The fact that it was a statement and not a question gave Lowell a funny feeling. The man had seen him before and knew who he was. He said, "Yes, sir, I'm on evenings."

"I believe you're Lyall?—"

"No, sir. Name Lowell Holbrook, Jr."

"Lila your sister?"

"Yes, sir, she is. She waits table in the dining room." He had never seen Son Martin in the dining room; he had only seen him those few times in the lobby talking to Mrs. Lyons; but the man surely knew things about the hotel.

"Holbrook." Son Martin was placing the name. "Your family used to farm over toward Caldwell."

"Yes, sir, till the floods washed us out." Lowell waited with Son Martin looking at him, then couldn't wait any more. "A year ago me and my sister come over here to live with kin and we was able to get these jobs."

Son Martin kept looking at him until finally he said, "You're here. You might as well stay to supper."

It took him by surprise and gave him the funny feeling again, though now it was funny another way. Here he was talking to Son and being invited to have supper with him. What was so scary or different about Son Martin? Lowell told him he'd had a fair-sized dinner and sure wished he could stay and eat, but he had to get to work.

Driving away he kept glancing at the rearview mirror, at Son Martin on the porch watching him. He didn't wave, just watched. There was no sign of the hounds, which was good. Going down the road through the thicket he remembered he should have asked Son how come Mr. Baylor was warning him about the raid. It didn't make sense, unless Son was paying off the sheriff. But that didn't make sense either. If it was the case Mr. Baylor would tell Son himself, he wouldn't have somebody else do it. People did crazy things where whiskey was concerned. It being against the law to drink wasn't going to stop anybody. They'd fight and shoot each other and go to prison and die for it, so there was no sense in wondering about Mr. Baylor and Son Martin.

It was a relief to see the opening in the scrub growth and the road below him. Lowell kept his foot on the brake feeling the car sliding in the mud, the rear-wheels banging from side to side in the ruts. He said, "Hold her, Bessie," and slapped the steering wheel around making his turn, and right then he had to cut hard to swerve to miss going head on into a car parked in the road. Not a car, a line of cars, four, *five* of them parked there with

7

the men standing strungout alongside and all of them now staring at him as he went by. Lowell kept going. He looked at the rearview mirror and saw the men and cars getting smaller as he pulled away from them; they were still watching him and some of them were out in the road now. He'd recognized a few of them, people from around here; but couldn't place their names.

He surely wished somebody would tell him what the hell was going on in this world.

Mr. Baylor never could adjust the goddamn field glasses right, so he let his deputy, E.J. Royce, work them. They were on a ridge above the Martin place where they could look down two hundred yards or so through the trees to the cleared land and the outbuildings and the weathered house and the wisp of smoke rising out of the chimney pipe.

"What're they doing now?" Mr. Baylor asked E.J. Royce. The old man squinted into the distance through steel-framed spectacles: a seventy-three-year-old turkey buzzard face beneath a farmer's straw hat; tight mouth barely moving and a hunk of plug stuck in his sunken cheek.

"The nigger just come out carrying something." E.J. Royce spoke with the field glasses pressed to his face. "A pan. There, he just throwed the dishwater out'n the yard. Now he's gone back inside."

"Son come out?"

"No, sir, he's still in the house."

"I want quiet over there," Mr. Baylor said. "If you people can't keep still, bite on your lip or go home."

Somebody must have said something funny, the men laughing and shaking their heads, then hushing up looking solemn as Mr. Baylor spoke to them: the group waiting a few yards back, in the trees. Mr. Baylor usually deputized these same men, selected from his circle of friends. But on a raid, watching a place or moving in on it, he always called them "you people."

One of them, standing up, said to Mr. Baylor, "He can't hear nothing from where he's at."

Mr. Baylor's steel-rimmed glare turned on the man. "How do you know he can't?"

"Hit's too far," the man said.

"You want to swear on a goddamn Bible he can't hear you? You going to tell me what he can hear and what he can't, living out here and knowing every sound?" Mr. Baylor was talking louder than the man had talked.

E.J. Royce listened, the field glasses to his eyes, waiting for Mr. Baylor to finish. One time, watching like this, he had said, "Mr. Baylor, the man knows we're coming. What difference is it if we make noise?" And Mr. Baylor's glasses glinted and flashed and his mouth went tight. "Because you don't make any noise on a raid," Mr. Baylor hissed. "That's why." He had been either a sheriff or some kind of county official for over thirty years, since before the year 1900, so he knew what he was talking about.

E.J. Royce said, "Son's come out of the house and gone in the privy."

Mr. Baylor jumped on him. "Well, god-damn-it, whyn't you tell me?"

"It's all right, he's in there."

"I'll tell you what's all right." Mr. Baylor looked over at the deputy group to make sure they'd heard. The waiting was an important part of it. Mr. Baylor would take out his time-piece and look at it and then look up at the sky. The men would watch as he did this and he would feel them watching.

"He's come out of the privy," E.J. Royce said.

Mr. Baylor squinted into the dusk. "Doing what?" He couldn't make out a thing down in the yard.

"Buttoning his pants," a man in the deputy group said, and there was a little sniggering sound from the rest of them.

Before Mr. Baylor could jump on the man, E.J. Royce said, "Now he's going toward his pickup truck," and felt Mr. Baylor close to him, the old man breathing, making a wheezing sound. "No, he's past it now, heading up the slope."

"Going to the grave," Mr. Baylor said.

"I reckon so. Yes, sir, that's what it looks like." E.J. Royce waited, holding the glasses on Son as he came up the gentle slope of the pasture. "He's near the grave now. Now he's stepped over the fence and is standing by the post."

Mr. Baylor was nodding. "Every evening. That's something, he does that."

10

"The light went on," E.J. Royce said. "You see it?"

"God Almighty, I'm not blind."

It was a small, cold light in the dusk, over a way, near the foot of a steep section of the slope, a hundred yards below them and over to the left: a single bulb under a tin shade that was fixed to the top of the nine-foot post. Mr. Baylor and his people could make out the low fence now and the grave marker and the single figure standing by the post.

"I didn't see him turn it on," E.J. Royce said.

"The switch is in the house," Mr. Baylor told him. "Aaron must've turned it on."

One of the men in the group said, "Hardly anybody has 'lectricity in their houses, Son uses it on a grave."

Mr. Baylor shot him a look. It was too dark for the look to do any good, but he put enough edge in his tone to make up for it. He said, "You work in a mine and die in a mine you appreciate a light on your grave, mister. You think about it."

The man said, "It ain't doing the old man any good."

And Mr. Baylor said, "How do you know that? Are you down there in the dirt looking up? How in hell would you know it ain't doing any good?" Jesus, people knew a lot.

E.J. Royce let him finish. "The nigger's come out of the house—going up toward the grave. Son's just standing there."

"Waiting for us," Mr. Baylor said. "It's time."

He led them down through the trees and laurel thickets, not saying anything now about the noise they were making. As they approached the pasture Mr. Baylor drew his .44 Colt revolver, pointed it up in the air, and fired it off.

Aaron looked off in that direction, toward the dark mass of the hill, and Son Martin said, "He's telling the rest of them down on the road."

From across the pasture they heard a second revolver report in the settling darkness.

"They anxious," the Negro said. "They don't want anybody miss nothing."

Son kept his eyes on a little spot way off and soon was aware of specks of movement taking shape, the men spread out as they crossed the pasture, some of them heading for the yard. In the barn the two fox-hounds began barking and yelping to get free. In a minute then, from the other side of the house, Son picked up the faint sound of the cars coming up the hollow.

Close to him Aaron said, "Company tonight, everybody welcome."

Son walked along the edge of the grave mound that was covered with stones, to be moving, doing something. He put his hands in his back pockets. It was getting chilly. Maybe he should have put on a coat. No, he'd be warm enough pretty soon. He said to Aaron, "You might as well get it out."

"How much you think?"

"Lay that part-full barrel on the porch, with some jars."

"Or give them some we cooked yesterday."

"No, out of the barrel tonight"

He could see them clearly now, most of them coming this way, a few straggling toward the yard. Headlight beams moved in the trees as the first car topped the rise out of the hollow. As the next cars followed, pulling into the yard, their headlights caught Aaron walking back to the house. Son waited for the group coming toward him. There weren't many bugs around the post light; it was still too cool. Another month he wouldn't be able to stand here for long they'd be so thick. Another month after that he wouldn't have to. He'd be gone.

Son looked down at the gravestone, at his shadow across the inscription.

John W. Martin
1867-1927
*May he rest ever
in the Lord's
Eternal Light*

He looked up at the repeated sounds of a car horn. Headlight beams crisscrossed the yard with dust hanging in the light shafts; there were voices now and the laughter of grown men out for a good time, the men from the cars yelling toward the ones coming across the pasture. Out of the darkness somebody called, "Hey, Son, you up there?"

He hesitated. "Waiting for you boys!"

Now he set a grin on his face, relaxed it, and set it again, ready to greet them as they came into the light. Then he was shaking E.J. Royce's hand and E.J. was saying, "Son, where you been keeping yourself?"

"I been right here all the time."

"I know you have—I mean how come you haven't been down to see us?"

"You know how it is."

"Sure, up here drinking your own whiskey. Well, a man makes it as fine as you do, I can't say as I blame you."

Mr. Baylor gave E.J. Royce a sharp-pointed elbow pushing between him and the man next to him. He waited as Son nodded, then said, straight-faced and solemn as he could, "Son Martin, we have reason to believe you are presently engaged in the manufacture and commercial sale of intoxicating liquor in violation of the Eighteenth Amendment of the United States Constitution. Is that true?"

"Yes, sir." Son nodded respectfully, going along.

"Then as sheriff of this county I order you to produce it," Mr. Baylor said, "before all these boys here die of thirst."

By the way people came in, Lowell could tell if they'd been to the Hotel Cumberland before. If they walked right over to the main desk, knowing it was back of the stairway and partly hidden, they'd been here. If they came in

14

and looked around the lobby and up at the high ceiling and the second floor balcony and weren't sure where to go, it was their first time.

But the man in the dark suit and hat, carrying the big leather suitcase, stumped Lowell: he didn't walk directly to the desk but he didn't gawk around either. He came in the entrance slowing his stride, holding the bag with a couple of hooked fingers, and seemed to locate the desk without looking for it. He walked over, set his suitcase down, and spread his hands on the counter.

Coming up next to him Lowell said, "Evening," reaching over then to palm the desk bell, hitting it twice. The man looked at him and nodded. He looked tired and needed a shave and was a little stoop-shouldered the way some tall men carry themselves.

Mrs. Lyons came out of the office that was behind the main desk. She said good evening in her quiet tone and opened the register. Mrs. Lyons always looked good, her dark hair was always parted in the middle and combed back in a roll without a wisp of loose hair sticking out. She was the neatest, cleanest-looking person Lowell had ever seen. (And he surely couldn't picture her in bed with Son Martin, or anybody.) He watched her now. Her eyes were something; they were dark brown. Sometimes they sparkled when she smiled and had the warmest look he had ever seen. Though sometimes—watching her closely when she was talking to another person—her face would smile, but her eyes would tell nothing: as if

15

she were looking at the person from behind her smile, or maybe thinking about something else. Whenever he talked to her for any reason, Lowell would have to look over somewhere else, once in a while. She was a lot older than he was, at least thirty, and he didn't know why he'd get the nervous feeling.

The man didn't take his hat off. He bent over and wrote slowly *Frank Long, Post Office Box 481, Frankfort, Ky.* Mrs. Lyons dropped her eyes and brought them back up and asked Mr. Long if he was staying just the night. He shook his head saying he wasn't sure how long he'd be; maybe just a few days. Mrs. Lyons didn't ask him anything else—if he was a salesman or here on some business or visiting kin. The dark eyes went to Lowell as she handed him the key to 205.

Lowell bent over to pick up Mr. Long's suitcase, then put his free hand on the counter as he straightened—God, like there was bricks in the thing. Mr. Long was watching him. He didn't say anything; he followed Lowell up the stairway.

In the room, putting the bag down and going over to the window, Lowell said, "You got a nice front view." He leaned close to the pane, seeing his own reflection over the lights and lit-up signs across the street. Frank Long was looking at himself in the dresser mirror, feeling his beard stubble.

Lowell said, "Can I get you anything else?"

"Like what?" Mr. Long asked

"I don't know. Anything you might feel

16

like." He waited as the man took off his coat and tie and started unbuttoning his shirt. "Did you want anything to drink?"

Mr. Long looked at him, pausing a second and holding the button. "Are you talking about soda pop or liquor?"

"Either," Lowell said. "Or both."

"You can get whiskey?"

"Maybe. There's a person I could call."

"Don't you know selling liquor's against the law?" He pulled off his shirt; a line of black hair ran up from his belt buckle and spread over his chest like a tree. His skin was bone white and hard muscled.

"I'm not saying I'd get it. I said maybe there was a person I could call."

"How late's the dining room open?"

"Till eight. You want something you'll have to hurry."

Mr. Long pulled a fold of bills from his pocket. He handed one to Lowell. "Tell them to dish up. I'll be down in ten minutes."

"Thank *you*," Lowell said. "Tonight they got breaded pork chops, chicken-fried steak, or baked ham."

"Ham," Mr. Long said. He let Lowell edge past and reach the door. Lowell was opening it when he said, "Boy, do you know a Son Martin?"

Lowell kept his hand on the knob. He came around slowly, giving himself time to get a thoughtful frown on his face. The man was unbuckling the straps of his suitcase. Lowell watched him let the two sections of the suitcase fall open on the bed.

17

As the man looked at him, Lowell said, "There's a Son Martin lives about ten miles from here. I don't know as it's the same one you mean though."

"How many Son Martins d'you suppose there are?"

"I guess I never thought to count them."

Frank Long studied him. "This one I know, his daddy was a miner before he passed on. Name John W. Martin. This Son—if it's the one—him and me soldiered together in the United States Army."

"You were in the war with Son?"

"In the Engineers if it's the same one."

"Well, it sure sounds like it. John W. was his papa's name."

"You say he lives about ten miles from here?"

"You go out the county road till you see the sign *Broke-Leg Creek*, turn left, second road about a mile or so you turn left again. That takes you right up the hollow where he lives."

The man smiled and it looked strange on his solemn, beard-stubbled face. He said, "Boy, you've been a big help to me." He waited a second and then said, "Hey, you want to see something?"

"What?"

"Something I got here." His big hand unsnapped the canvas cover on one side of the suitcase.

"What is it?"

"Come take a look."

It was strange, Lowell wasn't sure he wanted

18

to. He felt funny being alone in the room with this man.

"I got it strapped in or I'd take it out," Mr. Long said.

"Strapped in?" Lowell stepped toward the edge of the bed. He didn't know what to expect. Least of all he didn't expect to see a big heavy-looking army gun, polished wood and black metal and bullet clips, the gun broken down and each part tied and packed securely. Laying there on the bed with the overhead light shining on it. God. A real army gun they used in the war right there, he could touch it if he wanted to.

"God," Lowell said.

"You ever see anything like that?"

"Just pictures."

"You know what it is?"

"I think it's a BAR rifle."

"That's right," Mr. Long said. "Browning Automatic Rifle. U. S. Army issue." He let the canvas cover fall over the gun. "I expect not many around here have seen one."

"No sir." Lowell looked up at him now. He hesitated, then said it quickly, before he could change his mind, "What do you use a gun like that for?"

"Hunting," Mr. Long said. "For hunting."

Lowell didn't tell Mrs. Lyons about the gun. When he went downstairs he thought about telling her, but he didn't. Maybe it would make her nervous. If he was going to tell anybody, Lowell decided, it would be Mr. Baylor. Mr. Baylor would know what to do.

About a half hour later Lowell saw Frank Long come out of the dining room. He had his hat on and was lighting a cigar as he walked out of the front entrance. He didn't have the suitcase with him.

Lowell said to Mrs. Lyons, behind the desk, "There sure a lot of people interested in Son Martin lately."

She gave him a strange look. It was the closest he'd ever come to seeing something in her eyes.

two

There were twenty-three men at Son Martin's place that Saturday night. They were inside the house sitting around the table. They were on the porch where a coal oil lantern hung from a post and where Mr. Baylor's deputies had placed their firearms against the wall. Some were out by the cars. But most of them stayed close to the whiskey barrel that was at the edge of the porch, the spigot sticking out, so that from the ground a man would reach up to fill his fruit jar. They were quiet at first, taking their turns with the jars, sipping the whiskey, tasting it, and thinking about the taste as it burned down to their stomachs. The serious drinkers stood and squatted and spit tobacco on the hardpack at the dim edge of the porch light as though they were waiting for a meeting to start, or waiting out front of a mine company hiring shed: men in broad hats and engineer caps and worn-out suitcoats over their Duck Head overalls.

It was a clear night and not too cold and god*damn* that Son Martin could run whiskey. He let his mash set a full six or seven days and didn't put a lot of devilment in it, like buckeye beans or carbide or lye, to hurry up the fermentation. Son took his time; he cooked the beer slowly over a low fire; he used pure copper in the works and limestone spring water to condense the vapor and he kept his still clean. The clear moonshine that came out of the flake stand was run again, doubled through the works, and filtered through charcoal before it was put up to age and mellow in charcoal-blackened white oak barrels. Son aged his run two to four months, which he said was bare minimum to give it color. If you weren't willing to wait, you'd have to go somewhere else and drink clear moonshine. It was worth a wait, E.J. Royce said, because good whiskey was kinder to a person and didn't beat your brains out the next morning. The men E.J. Royce was talking to agreed a hundred per cent because they wanted to believe it. Though each man knew if he drank as much as he wanted, he'd feel the pain the next day like a wet leather strap shrinking into his head and his mouth would be stuck together with an awful sour glue taste and he'd drink a gallon of water and six cups of coffee and a couple of bottles of Nehi soda before noon. But tomorrow morning was tomorrow morning. Tonight they'd raided Son Martin's and they were here to drink and confiscate.

Mr. Baylor set aside five half-gallon jars as sheriff of this county and paid Son eight dollars—just about half the going rate—calling it the confiscation price. Mr. Baylor said he wasn't going to sit around all night with these punkin rollers, so he had his stuff put in a car early.

Bud Blackwell was here with his dad and his married brother Raymond. Bud said the whiskey was all right, but he'd tasted better. He said to his brother Raymond and to Virgil Worthman and a couple other boys, where they should be with the whiskey was in town, get themselves some girls, and have a real party instead of listening to the old men talking about closed-down mines and flooded bottom land and tight-assed Herbert Hoover and the goddamn banks. There were sweet girls down there in Marlett waiting, Bud Blackwell said. Jesus, sweet and ready. Or they could ride over to this place in Corbin, near the railroad tracks, where there were girls; he'd been over there with his dad one time—hell no, Raymond hadn't gone, not married a year yet. Bud opened his pocketknife and scratched a little circle in the hardpack and began flicking the knife at it sticking the blade every time.

Uncle Jim Bob Worthman, ten years older than Mr. Baylor, sat on the steps for a while drinking whiskey, then went up and took a shotgun from the porch and, swaying in the coal oil light, taking aim, let go both barrels at Son Martin's barn, saying he'd seen a Yankee up in the loft. Bud Blackwell said, Jesus, put that old man to bed before he starts telling about his war; there have been wars since that goddamn war of his. Virgil took Uncle Jim Bob over to their car and talked to him until he went to sleep in the back seat, telling the old man he'd cut the bluebelly dead center and that it was the best shooting ever seen. I hit my share at Lookout Mountain, the old man said. Virgil said, yes, sir, hoping Jim Bob hadn't shot one of Son's mules or one of his foxhounds.

Somebody asked Son if his radio played, they could listen to a program from Nashville. Son said, no, it hadn't worked in some time. The man said, you keep a light burning over a hole in the ground but your radio don't play. E.J. Royce told the man, quietly, to be careful talking about Son Martin's papa. Son takes it wrong. E.J. Royce said, he'll kick out all your teeth.

Then, changing the subject, E.J. Royce wondered that, if Son Martin made the best whiskey, who made the worst? He was just kidding. Moonshiners like the Blackwells and the Stampers and the Worthmans were always making fun of each other's whiskey. One of the moonshiners would say something now and they'd start funning each other. But it was a man on the porch who'd come with Mr. Baylor who said Christ, Arley Stamper; he puts mule piss in a jar and sells it as pure corn. Arley had been in the privy and was coming up the porch steps. He grinned at the man who said it and, as he reached the top step, hit the man full in the mouth with his right fist, took hold of him with his left hand, and hit him again and sent him off the porch. Arley Stamper looked down at the man on the ground and said to E.J. Royce, "E.J., who was that I hit?"

Bud Blackwell took a good drink of whiskey. Holding the fruit jar in front of him, he stared out at the darkness thoughtfully. Finally he nodded and said, "Speaking of mule piss, I wonder which one of Son's animals give us this run."

He didn't look up at Son, who was on the porch, but knew Son had heard him. He took another drink and licked his lips slowly, as if registering the aftertaste in his mind. "Either mule piss or John W. Martin whiskey," Bud Blackwell said. "I bet ten dollars."

Some of the others looked over, knowing what Bud was leading to. They looked up at Son as a stillness settled in the yard, then moved in closer as Son came down the steps toward Bud Blackwell. Bud handed Son the fruit jar and now they watched him raise it and take a long pull, wondering how much he'd already drunk. Nobody was sure what Son could hold; the only thing certain, no matter how much he put away, nobody had ever seen him talkative or loud or open with his thoughts. One time before it was Bud Blackwell who'd said, "The son of a bitch, he could get shitfaced and fall off his porch five times an evening and never say more'n ouch." But maybe this time was different and Son would open up. The word passed into the house Bud was fooling with Son and Mr. Baylor and the others at the table, including Bud's dad, came out to watch. Bud's dad was twisting his mustache and chuckling and shaking his head like it was all in fun, though inside he was nervous and hoping to hell Bud wouldn't get knocked on his ass.

Bud took the fruit jar from Son and held it up to the coal oil glow, facing the audience on the porch. "You claim you run this, is that right?"

Son was patient, knowing what was coming. He said, "I should know, shouldn't I?"

Bud cocked his head, studying the amber inches of whiskey in the jar. "Son, was you taking this to the vet?"

That got some sounds from the people. Mr. Blackwell laughed out loud and then shut his mouth. Son kept quiet.

"Yeah, I see specks of some in there," Bud said. "Like little bugs. Them bugs, Son?"

There was nothing for Son to get angry about, but there was no reason to stand grinning at Bud Blackwell either. He said, "What you're saying, it was either a sick mule run it or else my dad." Son spoke mildly, but it was clear he was laying it out between them and taking Bud head on. He said, "You either want your skull busted or you want to rile me into claiming my dad made the best whiskey in east Kentucky. Once I do you say, if that's true, prove it. And I say Bud, how can I prove it if he's dead in his grave?"

Bud Blackwell grinned. "That's getting us there. Then I say—go on, you're doing fine—what do I say?"

"You say let's quit talking about the whiskey and drink it."

"Pig's ass I do."

"You say I must be getting drunk cause I'm sure running off at the mouth—I think my daddy better tuck me in bed."

That got some sounds with E.J. Royce saying, "Tell him Son," and Mr. Blackwell giving E.J. a dirty look. They were watching Bud Blackwell to see what he'd do now, with his mouth tight and no sign of it curling into a grin. But Bud never got his turn.

Aaron appeared out of the darkness, moving through the group in the yard, not saying excuse me or anything until he was next to Son. There he was, barely giving them time to wonder where he came from or what he wanted. Aaron said, "Somebody coming in a car."

Frank Long was aware of the whole scene at once, like walking into a dark room and having the lights go on and everybody yelling surprise. He came up out of the hollow and there were the cars and the house and the men gathered in the dim glow of the porch lamp. The difference was nobody yelled surprise. They stood waiting for him, not making a sound. Long sat in his car a few moments, aware now of the spot of light up on the hill over a mound, over something; he didn't know what it was or much care right now. The men were waiting and if it was a party it surely wasn't in his honor. He couldn't back out now and turn around, so he got out and walked between the cars and when he was in the open, spotting the whiskey barrel now, he said, "I'm looking for John W. Son Martin, Jr. Am I at the right place or have I interrupted a church meeting?"

As a couple of them moved aside there was Son.

Long stopped before he reached the light. He let an easy grin form as he said, "Hey, Son, don't you recognize an old buddy?"

Son couldn't see his face in the dark, but he said, "Frank Long," and saw the man from another time, Frank Long in uniform and leggings and the brim of his campaign hat curling up in front.

Son wanted to act natural and glad to see him; he wanted to raise his voice to match Long's and get that friendly sound in it and hand him a jar and slap him on the shoulder a couple of times and say, "Frank, you old son of a bitch, it's been four years, hasn't it? Summer of 1927, Camp Taylor"—and act like nothing better could have happened than Frank Long appearing out of the dark. Except that the moment he heard Long's voice and felt his stomach knot up, he knew why the man was here.

Son said, "Frank, step over where we can see you."

Frank Long came into the light holding his

grin. "You recognized my voice, didn't you? Well, I guess you should, we was in the same tent, how long?"

"Fifteen months."

"That's right, nearly a year and a half. Son, I'd known your voice too. Jesus, I heard it singing and telling stories enough, didn't I?"

"Well, not too much."

"You tell these boys stories, Son?"

Goddamn him, what was he doing? Son forced a grin and said, "Listen, what I want to know—I thought you were still in."

"Mustered out last fall. I had a bellyful of it."

"I was wondering what—"

But Mr. Baylor, at the top of the steps, called out just loud enough to get their attention, "Son, we never known you was a singer."

Son glanced up. "He means with the other boys in the outfit."

"Oh, I thought maybe you'd sing us a song." Mr. Baylor kept watching him. He could see it or sense it—he wasn't sure which—that Son was holding back and didn't feel comfortable in this man's presence. Son knew something about the man. Or else the man knew something about Son. Mr. Baylor was curious and he was old enough that he could be blunt and not care what anybody thought.

He said, "Mr. Long, my name is Mr. Baylor and I'm sheriff of this county. Where abouts are you from?"

Frank Long touched the funneled brim of his dark hat. "Well, sir, I'm from all over the state, you might say."

"I might not" Mr. Baylor said, "I'm asking you where you're from."

"Most recently? I guess that would be Frankfort."

"They say it's a pretty town, though I've never been there," Mr. Baylor said. "Tell me, what do you do in Frankfort?"

"I work for the government."

"Is that the state government?"

"No, Sir, the United States Federal Government."

"I see," Mr. Baylor said. "Well now I add up all that information and you know what it tells me?

"No, sir, what?"

"It tells me you're a Prohibition agent."

Frank Long stared up at him. "That's pretty good, Mr. Baylor, you got a keen eye, haven't you?"

"And nose," Mr. Baylor said. "Let's see your credentials."

Long reached into his back pocket for his billfold. Flipping it open he said, "They give me this—card with my picture on it. Not a good likeness though. And they give me Sweetheart." His right hand came from inside his coat gripping a .45-caliber service automatic. He glanced at Son and the men watching him. "You never see one like this? I know Son has in the Army. This beauty will stop a man in his tracks and set him back five paces."

"Boy," Mr. Baylor said to him then, "are you threatening anybody?"

"You asked me for my credentials."

"I see them," Mr. Baylor said. "You see mine up there leaning against the wall. Shotguns and high-powered rifles."

"Yes, Sir."

"Any law needs upholding in this county, I take care of it."

"I see that too," Long said, his gaze sliding over to the whiskey barrel. "All these people here your deputies?"

Mr. Baylor was as courteous and nice as anyone had ever seen him. He said, "Yes, they are, and I'll tell you something. They ain't ever seen a Prohibition agent before."

"Is that right?"

"Yes," Mr. Baylor went on, "a revenue man is a rare bird in this county. I mean it's so rare some old boy sees one, you know what he's liable to do?"

"What's that?"

"He's liable to shoot it and have it stuffed and put over his fireplace."

Frank Long shook his head, grinning. "Man, I don't think that would feel so good, getting stuffed."

Bud Blackwell felt it was time he got into this. He said, "You know what we stuff them with?"

But Mr. Baylor wasn't having any Bud Blackwell smart-ass talk right now. He didn't need any Bud Blackwells sticking their nose in his business. He said, "Bud, get Mr. Long a drink of whiskey."

Frank Long looked appreciative. "Well, if you force me to take one."

Mr. Baylor waited until Long was handed a jar and watched him drink some of it. "Kind of good, isn't it?"

"This is all right," Long said, nodding, studying the jar.

"It'd be a shame to pour it on the ground," Mr. Baylor said. "Wouldn't it? Just cause some dried up titless old women don't believe people should drink whiskey."

"Isn't that the truth?" Long finished the whiskey and wiped the back of his hand across his mouth. "Mr. Baylor, as you say, a man is paid to uphold the law. But that don't mean he can't appreciate the finer things in life."

Mr. Baylor said, "Have another drink, Mr. Long."

"I don't mind." He handed the jar to Bud Blackwell for a refill and waited for Bud to take it. "No, sir, you had me wrong. I was passing through, I thought I'd stop and visit is all."

Mr. Baylor adjusted his steel frame spectacles. "I was going to say before, maybe you ought to get your visiting done and start back to Frankfort before it gets too late."

"Well, it's up to Son." Long looked over at him. "I got me a room at the hotel for a day or two."

"It's a good one," Mr. Baylor said. "Hotel Cumberland."

"It seems nice and clean."

"Good food in the dining room. Say, have you had your supper?"

Long hesitated. "Well, I had me a little something."

"Son," Mr. Baylor said, "Your friend here's hungry. That's a long car ride from Frankfort.

"Don't be nervous these boys here staring at you. As I said they never seen a federal man close up."

Long grinned, shaking his head. "Listen, underneath this suit there's just a plain old mountain boy. I did most of my growing up down in Harlan County."

"Is that right?"

"Yes, sir, till I went in the U. S. Army."

"Son," Mr. Baylor said, "you going to have Aaron fix something?"

Son was staring at Frank Long and had been looking at him since the moment he heard the man's voice in the darkness and felt the tight little warning stab deep in his belly. He had listened to Long and Mr. Baylor, every word, as the two of them warmed up and relaxed and if Son wanted to he could pretend everything was just swell and talk and smile and wait for Frank Long—some other time, not this evening—to start hinting and leading up to it, the way Bud Blackwell had started fooling with the idea just a little earlier. Or he could push it in Frank Long's face right now, call him and get it out in the open.

Or, he could think about it some more, not being hasty and maybe regretting it.

Yes, he could think about it and waste time and lose his nerve and in a few minutes he'd be grinning and nodding at everything the son of a bitch said and his face would begin to ache from the grinning. So do it, Son decided. Jesus, do it, will you?

Still looking at the man, he said, "Frank didn't come here to eat supper."

Long's eyes opened, momentarily startled, then his expression settled and he watched Son calmly.

"He didn't come here to visit or talk about old times," Son went on. "He came here to find my dad's whiskey."

Some of the men looked at each other, hardly believing it. Mr. Baylor said, "That old story. Never mind that, Son. Let's get your friend here fed."

"He's not hungry for anything to eat." Son kept his gaze on Long. "He's got on his mind a hundred and fifty barrels of whiskey that's going to come of age this summer—a hundred and fifty barrels of eight-year-old John W. Martin corn whiskey. Isn't that right, Frank?"

Long said nothing; there was no silence for him to fill because Mr. Baylor was already pressing in. He said, "Hell, folks have heard that story and forgot it a hundred times. Who's going to prove John Martin ever put away any whiskey? Son, if he run that much and it's unaccounted for then your daddy drank it is all. Why I remember him drinking two-three gallon a week, drunk it 'stead of water. These boys all know that."

Some of them nodded and E.J. Royce said, "Why he'd a sure drunk it afore he ever hid it."

"No," Mr. Baylor said, "that's a story nobody can prove as fact."

Son was patient. He waited and said to Mr. Baylor, "I appreciate it. But Frank already knows about the whiskey."

"I suppose he's heard the story, sure," Mr. Baylor said, "same as everybody else. But that don't make it true."

Son waited again; there was no hurry. He said, "The difference is he heard it from me. One time in Louisville we'd gone in from Camp Taylor, I told him the whole story." Son paused, looking from Frank Long to Mr. Baylor. "You want to know something else? Soon as I told Frank, a second after, I knew I should have bit off my tongue and I started telling myself it was all right because he was probably too drunk to remember any of it. But you know what? Right then, back of some stores in the dark where we'd been doing our drinking, I knew some day Frank was going to come looking for the whiskey."

Nobody said anything. Son's gaze moved slowly from the porch, past the men in the yard to Frank Long. He waited a moment before saying, "But Frank's not going to get it. Not Frank or anybody."

three

They said it was toward the end of 1922 and into 1923 that Son Martin's father ran his hundred and fifty barrels of top-grade moonshine and put it away to age a full eight years.

They said he must have been planning it because he bought his white oak barrels three or four years before he ran the whiskey, bought them used at the time the Prohibition law closed the distilleries. They said John W. Martin put up the whiskey as an insurance policy. The old man wasn't going to buy any government Liberty bonds for savings, because it was the government that had taken Son into the Army and lured him into staying after the war was over. He wasn't giving the goddamn government anything. But he would have something to give Son once he got tired of marching around Camp Taylor playing soldier boy. Something worth more than any paper Liberty bonds.

Maybe the old man had put away the whiskey, maybe he hadn't. All anybody knew was the old man and Aaron and some kin of Aaron's had kept three stills working every day for a year. They'd seen the smoke curling out of the yellow pines above the Martin place and they knew he didn't sell more than a few dozen half-gallon jars during that time.

So, people said, he must have put it away: probably down a mine hole somewhere. While he was stilling, the old man mined coal more than he'd farmed and they said it must have been part of his plan: dig shafts to hide the barrels in, then cover them up with brush. As a final twist of the story, it was a mine that killed the old man, collapsed and suffocated him to death, not two months after Son had come home from the Army.

Mr. Baylor explained this to Frank Long in the Hotel Cumberland dining room late Sunday morning, Mr. Baylor watching Long eating his fried eggs and ham and hominy and finally calling Lila Holbrook over and ordering a plate for himself, with some hot coffee.

"I want you to understand it," Mr. Baylor said and waited.

Long's eyes raised from his fork. "Understand what?"

"Here's a man had a farm and a nice family, a married son helping him work the farm, two daughters married and living in Tennessee. Everything's just fine till the war come along. Son goes in the Army in 1918. The next year Son's wife, Elizabeth, and his mother both die of the influenza, both of them within a week of each other. Son decides to stay in the Army and the old man is alone."

Frank Long dipped his biscuit in the runny egg yellow. "What's there to understand?"

"I mean the old man working and hoping all these years."

"While Son was taking it easy in the Engineers."

This wasn't something he understood clearly or was sure he could explain, but Mr. Baylor

36

said, "Son had his own reason for staying in, not wanting to come home to an empty house."

"He never talked about his wife any."

"He never talks much about anything," Mr. Baylor said. "That's his way. His daddy was like that. What I'm saying now, what the daddy worked so hard for was *his*, his to sell or leave to Son or drink it all himself if he felt like it. Which is what might've happened."

"I reckon you have all kinds of theories," Long said.

"Why they could have sent it to market for all anybody knows."

"A hundred and fifty barrels?"

"There's ways. They could've paid somebody and shipped it out by railroad, hidden down in some coal. Next time you see it it's in a warehouse in Cleveland, Ohio."

"But they didn't," Long said. "They left it to age the eight years."

Mr. Baylor put on a laugh. The steel frames of his spectacles glinted as he shook his head. "I see you don't know anything about whiskey. Four years, eight years, what's the difference in the taste?"

"Maybe nothing, but if the customer believes eight-year-old is better he'll pay for it, won't he?"

"All right," Mr. Baylor said. "Nobody around here has ever seen a trace of that whiskey. Some boys have looked for it. I mean as a game, to see if they could find it, not to steal it. If it's there, it's Son's and nobody else's. Now these smart boys have prowled Son Martin's tract for years and they haven't smelled out a single jar of anything the old man run."

"Then they haven't looked in the right place." Long cleaned his plate with a piece of biscuit and stuck it in his mouth. "Or they come on it and not said anything."

"I'd known," Mr. Baylor said.

"I reckon you're going to keep talking as long as I sit here."

Mr. Baylor hesitated and came in from another direction. "You claim to be his friend?"

"If he don't mind my working for the U. S. Government."

"All right, if you're his friend, what'd you tell on him for?"

"They already knew." Long saw Mr. Baylor squinting at him, looking him straight in the eye. He said, "If a hundred people around here know it, a hundred here to Frankfort can know it too."

"You're telling me the federal authorities know about Son's whiskey and they sent you to find it?"

"That's what I'm saying."

"What're you going to tell your superior?"

"I haven't looked yet, so there's nothing yet to tell."

"Tell them it was a story somebody made up. I seriously advise it."

Long sucked at his teeth. He pulled a cigar out of his breast pocket and bit off the end. "Mister, I believe you told me you're a law officer."

Mr. Baylor was ready. "And I believe you

told me that don't stop a man from enjoying the finer things in life. Well, let me put it this way," Mr. Baylor said. "People around here have built their stills and drunk whiskey for more than a hundred years. They believe if a man plows the ground and sows it and raised corn, it's not the place of another man to tell him he can eat it but he can't drink it. That's what we think of your Prohibition law."

"I'm sorry to hear that," Long said easily. "You know I can call on you to help me if I want. I got authority to use you and all the deputies I need."

"You see how many you get."

"Well, I don't know." Long drew on the cigar and exhaled the smoke in a long slow stream. "I was thinking I'd get me some of the stillers to help me."

Mr. Baylor stared at him. "Like the Blackwells and the Stampers maybe?"

"Anybody operating stills."

"I want to be there when you ask them."

"Mister," Long said, "I'm not going to ask. I'm going to tell them. They help me find Son's whiskey or I start busting their stills."

"You got a short memory from last night. Once Son told why you'd come, there was some of them would have shot you full of holes and put you under." Mr. Baylor straightened and was silent as Lila Holbrook placed his breakfast in front of him. He wasn't sure now he wanted it; he'd already eaten breakfast at home. He saw Frank Long looking up and smiling and shaking his head when Lila asked if he cared for anything else. As she moved away, Mr. Baylor said, "You think about it, you'll recall I got you out of there last night. If I hadn't been there they'd have shot you or run you off in the woods nekked and that's a fact."

"They saw my gun," Long said. "If a man had drawn a pistol they'd have seen it again."

"Well, a cocky boy like you, I guess you could bust stills all by yourself."

"Or call Frankfort for help," Long said.

"Tell me something." Mr. Baylor was looking him straight in the eye again. "What do you get out of this? You get a five-dollar-a-month raise? Or they see what a sweet boy you are, they make you state Prohibition director?"

"That'd be something, wouldn't it?"

"Or, you've done your arithmetic and you see a hundred and fifty thirty-gallon barrels, that's—"

"Forty-five hundred gallons," Long said.

"At five bucks a gallon." Mr. Baylor paused, staring across the table at him. "Twenty-two thousand dollars. That right?"

"A little more."

"And the bootlegger he could make, I reckon a *hundred* and twenty-something thousand. That the figure you get?"

Long shook his head. "Not if I capture it. Poured on the ground, the figure comes to zero."

"Would it please you to see that?" Mr. Baylor asked. "What I mean to say, what is it makes you happy about doing this job?"

"I don't get anything more out of it than my pay."

"Then you must want to see some good boys without a means of making a living and watch their little children go hungry. You want to take food off their table and see them get cholera and rickets. Is that it? Listen, I'll tell you something, boy, they used to farm, every one of them, but on the night of May 30, four years ago, it started to rain—"

"Jesus, I know about the floods."

"Goddamn-it, I said it started to rain, I mean rain like it never rained before, all night it never stopped. The creeks overrun and filled the hollers and washed out timber and crops and livestock and roads and houses that had stood a hundred years. Now you can replace those things, but it also peeled away all the topsoil and that you don't replace. You don't grow a market crop on limestone either, or in wore-out pasture fields. So you grow a little corn for stilling and buy whatever other grain you need and pray God some drunken boy don't come along and shoot holes in your cooker. I'm saying, without stills some people around here would starve to death."

Frank Long was looking past Mr. Baylor's left shoulder, through the wide opening of the doorway into the lobby. He said, "That Mrs. Lyons is a good-looking woman, isn't she?"

Mr. Baylor leaned into the table; he moved aside the cold eggs he didn't want anyway. "Did you listen to what I was telling you?"

"Something about it raining," Long said.

"Mister, excuse me, will you?" He got up and left the dining room.

Lowell Holbrook was in the lobby emptying ash trays and picking up the Sunday paper from chairs. He'd traded shifts with the day bellboy so the boy could go somewhere. If Lowell hadn't traded he wouldn't be standing in the lobby with Frank Long coming toward him. He didn't know what to do. He didn't want to talk to the man because he was afraid he'd be nervous and maybe say the wrong thing. But it was too late to pretend he hadn't seen Mr. Long looking this way and raising his head as a sign he wanted him.

Frank Long didn't wait but came over to him. "Didn't I see Mrs. Lyons a minute ago?"

"She left," Lowell said.

"What do you mean she left?"

"I guess she wasn't feeling good. She went home a little early."

"Doesn't she live in the hotel?"

"No, sir. She did for a while. Then she rented herself a little house." Damn—he hadn't wanted to say *sir*. It just slipped out.

"You say rented herself. Don't she live with her husband?"

"No, sir." There it was again. "I guess her husband's dead."

"That's too bad," Mr. Long said. He turned without another word and walked out. Lowell moved over to the door and saw him get in his car.

Now what was he up to?

Talking to him hadn't been so bad. Except the calling him *sir*. Earlier that morning Lowell had called Mr. Baylor from the office when no one was there and told him about the BAR rifle in Frank Long's suitcase and the man saying he used it for hunting.

"I reckon he does," Mr. Baylor had said.

"Wouldn't a gun like that be against the law?"

"Not if you are the law yourself."

Mr. Baylor had told him then that Frank Long was a federal man. "Everybody will know it soon enough," Mr. Baylor had said. "But, Lowell, they don't have to know anything about that gun. All right?"

From the hotel entrance Lowell watched Frank Long drive off down the street, the same way Mrs. Lyons had gone. He thought about the BAR rifle again, upstairs in the room. He pictured himself going up to 205, opening the door with a passkey, and walking out with the whole suitcase.

Then what would he do with it?

There he'd be coming down the stairs as Frank Long walked into the lobby and looked up at him.

No, sir, there were things that were exciting to think about, but nobody with a brain in his head would ever do them in real life.

Frank Long spotted Mrs. Lyons before she was three blocks from the hotel. There, looking at the drugstore window, then moving along to the corner and into the noon sunshine, her dark hair taking on a glint of light: she looked fresh and probably smelled nice, took soapy baths with something in the water like perfume. A good-looking woman with a soft, warm body. Yes, sir, Frank Long decided. He watched her until she was in the next block, then gave the car some gas, got up to her, and swung in close to the curb.

"Mrs. Lyons?" He waited for her to look over. "Hop in, I'll give you a lift."

She didn't recognize him immediately. As she did she said, "Oh, I'm almost there, thank you."

"I don't see any houses along this street."

"The next street where you see the church? I live just up the hill back of there. Say"—now she put a little hint of surprise in the soft, southern-gentlewoman tone of her voice— "how do you know where I'm going?"

"I understand you're not feeling so good."

"I'm just tired I think."

"Then get in, I'll take you."

"Thank you—but I think the fresh air and sunshine will do me more good than any-thing."

Frank Long grinned at her. "It ain't going to make you look any better than you do."

"Well, thank you very much." Kay Lyons nodded politely and smiled, then let the smile fade as she turned away from him and continued on, hearing the car engine idling at the curb. She wasn't going to look back; not yet. She took her time and didn't glance over her shoulder

44

until she reached the corner. He was still sitting in the car.

Still there as she turned the corner and crossed the street diagonally toward the Baptist Church and walked up the road past the churchyard and the fenced-in cemetery. She knew he was going to follow her, in the car or on foot, to see where she lived. There was nothing she could do about it. If he came to her house and knocked on the door she wouldn't answer. She was tired of smiling and being polite to salesmen and railroad agents and timber buyers in their muddy high-laced shoes: ten hours a day at the hotel, being bright and efficient. If she didn't smile or get a little sparkle in her eyes or make herself laugh—if she just acted natural—they say, "What's the matter with *her*?"

Kay had the feeling her life was slipping by, leaving no more than a few fading pictures in her mind. She saw herself as a little girl, little Kay Worthman, shy and skinny and scared to death of her cousin Virgil. She saw a pretty girl in high school, her hair marcelled into tight curls, honor student, and secretary of her graduating class. She saw the bright, neatly dressed young lady with the good position in the hotel office, assistant to the manager when she met Alvin Lyons, who came through Marlett once a month with his sample case of drugs and pharmaceuticals. She had dated Alvin Lyons whenever he came to town: thirteen dates with him before they became engaged and eleven more before she married Alvin in the

Old Regular Baptist Church and left Marlett as Kay Lyons.

The next five years were fading pictures of her life in Louisville:

The red brick duplex on the street of two-family houses; she saw the house in the fall, when it was raining.

The garage that was empty all week with Alvin on the road.

The library books on the coffee table and the bedstand.

The movie theater three blocks from the house; the Ritz it was called.

Alvin coming home with his sample case late Friday evening, the tired smile and the kiss before he took off his hat and coat.

Alvin studying his correspondence course in business every Saturday afternoon at the dining-room table.

Alvin leaving the house every Monday morning before it was light; leaving it the last time.

Finding him in the tightly closed darkness of the garage, lying beneath the car's rumbling exhaust pipe, his body wedged against the double doors.

The last picture of Alvin Lyons was clear and perhaps it would never fade. Kay would see him lying on the oil-stained cement and sometimes she would want to shake him until his eyes opened and say to him, "Why did you do it? Why did you let me think everything was going to be all right? Why did you let me give you six years and then kill yourself?"

She was back where she had started, as bright and efficient as before, now manager of the hotel.

But she was also thirty-one years old and she didn't want to be bright and efficient in the service of others or the manager of a county seat hotel. She wanted to be herself and not have to concern herself with people. She wanted someone to take care of her, someone who was as sensitive and perceptive as she was, someone she could rely on and trust and know would always be there. It seemed so simple. She just wanted everything to be *right*.

The house she had rented for thirty-five dollars a month wasn't at all right. It was dismal inside and smelled old and the floors creaked. The only good points, it was a comfortable walk from the business district and it was private: a tiny one-bedroom place that had once been a tenant farmhouse, sheltered by cedars and overlooking rolling pasture fields out of the back windows.

Crossing the ditch to the front yard, Kay looked back the way she had come, far down the empty gravel road to the cemetery and the red-brick church standing on the corner. There was no sign of him. Soon though, she was sure, a car would drive slowly past the house. The car would turn around and come back and this time would stop.

Kay let herself in the front door. She did not seem outwardly surprised or startled to see Son Martin in the easy chair, but as she closed the door behind her she said, "God, you scared me. I didn't see your truck."

Son had lowered the newspaper and was looking at her from the chair. "It's in the shed. Hey, you're early, aren't you?"

"You were behind the paper," Kay said, "I don't know why, I had a funny feeling you were going to be someone else."

"How many keys to this place did you give out?"

"I mean it. It was an awful feeling."

"Listen, I brought most of a quart jar—if you want something to relax."

"He followed me," Kay said. "Frank Long."

She stared at Son until he got up from the chair and moved to the front window. Looking out, holding open the curtain, he said, "I guess you know who he is and about last night."

"In the lobby this morning," Kay said, "people were talking about it who don't even know you."

"By now I bet it's a good story." Son leaned close to the glass pane to see down the road.

"They say he got Mr. Baylor and his men to help raid your still."

"I don't see a car."

"He's there," Kay said, "somewhere. He wanted to give me a ride."

"What kind of a car was it?"

"I don't know. A Ford, I think. He stopped me on the street."

Son looked around as she came over to stand close to him. He smiled a little and said, "Well, sure he would."

"He was in the dining room just before I left. Mr. Baylor came in and they talked for quite a while."

"Have you talked to Frank?"

"No. Only when he registered last night and a few minutes ago."

"Did he tell you he knew me?"

"I heard that this morning. When you were in the Army."

"We weren't good friends, but sometimes we'd go out and have some drinks." Son shook his head, thinking about it. "I've drunk too much with people before, but I never told anybody but him. Kay, why do you suppose I told him?"

"I don't know. I guess because you trusted him."

"I didn't have any reason to. You know, I don't think I even liked him especially. But I told him, the only person I ever told."

"You told me."

"You already knew about it. Like everybody around here."

"But I never thought about it," Kay said. "It didn't mean anything to me until now."

Son half turned from the window, "Listen, why don't we get a little more comfortable."

"What if he comes?"

He touched her hip and slid his arm around her waist. "What if he does?"

"Should I answer the door?"

"We won't worry about it this minute." Son could feel the satin slip beneath her blouse and the edge of her ribs beneath the slip-

49

pery feeling of the satin. Close to his shoulder her brown eyes were watching him, trusting him, and he could feel her breast and hip pressed against his side, the grown woman with the innocent little girl expression. He said, "If you want to take off your shoes or anything, I'll pour us a couple."

She nodded slowly. "Just a weak one. It might make me feel better."

"That's what I was thinking."

"There's a bottle of ginger ale in the icebox."

Son nuzzled her ear and brushed his mouth across her cheek. "There isn't anything we have to worry about. Not anything." He heard her breath come out softly, then kissed her, holding his hand gently against her face.

In the kitchen Son poured whiskey into two glasses, adding ice-cold ginger ale to Kay's. He drank most of the whiskey in his own glass and half-filled it again. Now Son washed his face and hands at the sink and, with a wet hand, slicked his hair down to the side. Drying off with the dish towel he decided to have another pull. This one he took directly from the quart jar. It tasted better out of the jar; it was a strange thing but it was true. Already he could feel the warmth of the whiskey inside him. He felt good.

All morning he'd felt more alive and sure of himself than he'd felt in a long time. He would probably tell Kay or she would notice it. But if she asked him why, he wasn't sure he could explain it.

Frank Long was the cause. (Tell her *that*.)

Because if Frank hadn't walked in out of the dark, Son was sure he would still be smiling with his mouth closed and being nice to people when he didn't want to be. Bud Blackwell might be partly responsible. Bud had started in on John W. Martin whiskey and it had got Son up on the edge. But it was seeing Frank Long that got him to wipe the dumb smile off his face once and for all and say it out loud.

He felt good because now there wasn't anything bottled up inside him, making him afraid to open his mouth. He had admitted to Frank Long in the presence of more than twenty men that his dad had ran off the whiskey and put it away. They might have known or suspected it before; that didn't count. Now it was official. Admitting it was telling them straight it was a fact and they might as well quit playing with each other. He had the whiskey and they didn't and that's the way it was. They could fool around if they wanted, but if anybody got serious or got close he'd blow them off with a 12-gauge. Son hadn't said all that last night, but admitting the fact of the whiskey was like saying it and he would tell it again to Frank and to as many revenue agents as Frank cared to bring. They could all go home or to hell or hang around here and try Son Martin out; it didn't matter which.

That was the way he felt now, one o'clock Sunday afternoon, picking up two whiskey drinks in the kitchen of Kay's house and taking them into the bedroom.

She had drawn the shade and was standing

in her slip, holding the edge of the shade inches from the window, looking outside. When Son was next to her she said, "I don't see any sign of him." She took the drink and sipped it, holding the glass with both hands, looking up at Son's face.

He said, "Don't think about him. All right?"

"I can't help it."

"He's not going to bother us."

"It's just—feeling him out there."

"He's probably gone away."

"I hope so."

"Listen, why don't we hurry up and finish these?"

He liked her in a slip. He liked her in a slip knowing there was nothing beneath the smooth cloth but her body. He liked pulling the slip up over her hips and seeing her a little bit at a time. He liked it especially this time of day, the house silent and the sunlight flat against the window shade.

He was aware of the quiet afternoon bedroom and was aware of his brown arm and hard sucked-in belly and was aware of the woman nakedness of her pale skin and dark hair, aware that she was with and around him but also down in alone somewhere behind tightly closed eyes, seeing whatever she was feeling or thinking. He closed his eyes and was aware of a prickle of sweat across his shoulders and after he was down in there with her somewhere holding on and not aware of anything but being where he was at that moment with his eyes closed tight and trying to make it last, until finally it was quieter in the room than it had been quiet before.

Close to him, almost whispering, Kay said, "Hold me."

"What am I doing?"

"I mean *hold* me."

"Like that?"

"Yes, That's better."

"My arm wasn't right."

"Hold me tighter."

"How about right there?"

"Just hold me."

"You smell good."

"Tighter."

"I don't want to hurt you."

She worked her body tightly against his and lay still.

"I want to hold you, and be held by you every night. Pretty soon we'll be able to."

There was silence. Son opened his eyes, his face against her cheek, his gaze on the sunlight framed in the window. "Pretty soon," he said.

"Maybe in just a few weeks. Let's start thinking about it," she said. "See if we can set a date."

"Kay"—Son paused—"why all of a sudden?"

She opened her eyes and moved her head so she could look at him. "Because all of a sudden we don't have to stay in Marlett. There's nothing keeping us now. We can be married and live anywhere we want."

"We can get married and live up at my place, but you say you won't do it."

"Because if we set up housekeeping here, we'll stay here, I know it. I don't want to grow a little vegetable garden and watch you make illegal whiskey. I want to leave here while we have a chance before you think of some reason to stay."

"I've got the same reason I've always had. Maybe I'm dumb or something, but what's changed?"

She frowned, puzzled. "They've found your dad's whiskey."

"Nobody's found it."

"They know you've got it. Once they take the whiskey, there isn't any reason for you to sit up there in your hollow like an old mountaineer. You've said it yourself, the sooner you can leave Marlett, the better."

"Kay, nobody's found the whiskey. I'm going to sell it and make the money, and then we're going to leave here and buy good farmland or a business somewhere, I don't know which or where we're going. All I know right now is they don't have any idea where that whiskey is located. They've looked, but in eight years nobody's found it."

Kay pushed herself up on one elbow. "Son, this isn't a game any more you play with your neighbors. Frank Long is a federal officer."

"You're sure built. Look at them things."

"Honey, if you don't tell them where it is they can make it hard for you and send you to prison."

"They can do that quicker if I do tell them."

"But you didn't make it, your father did."

"That doesn't mean anything. He made it, but I got it. Thing is, they have to prove I got it." Son smiled a little. "They have to find it—Frank Long does. That's one man, and I don't know as he's any better at it than Bud Blackwell or your cousin Virgil or some of the other boys."

"I don't know why you don't see it." She was concerned, worried, and now a hint of anger crept into her voice. "You're dealing with the federal government, not just one man. He'll bring all the officers he needs and if they don't find it they can sit up in the hills forever and watch you, and you won't ever be able to sell the whiskey yourself. Don't you see that?"

"I see a man named Frank Long," Son said. "He's the only one I see and as yet I don't know what he has in mind. I mean I don't know if he's out looking for the government or just for Frank Long, and that makes a difference."

Kay said, "What if we went away for a while—a month or maybe even longer, go somewhere and then come back and see—" She stopped. Son had pressed a finger to his lips. He was looking at her but listening to something else, she could tell. Kay heard the sound then, through the living room and outside: someone on the front porch.

Son rolled away from her, off the bed. He felt funny walking out of the room without a stitch of clothes on. He sucked in his stomach and moved carefully, feeling Kay watching him. Son waited in the front room, listening, before he walked over to the front window. He didn't see anyone on the porch or in the yard but, as he waited, listening, he heard a car engine start, beyond the stand of cedars. A moment later the sound faded to nothing down the road. Son walked back to the bedroom.

Kay was sitting up in bed, holding the sheet in front of her. "Was it him?"

"I didn't see anybody."

"What if he was looking in the window?"

Son stepped into his pants. "He might have learned a new trick or two."

four

Before Son was all the way through Marlett, heading out the highway in his pickup truck, he knew Frank Long was following him—a black Ford coupe hanging back there, keeping its distance. If it wasn't Frank Long he didn't know who it was, so he'd take for granted it was Frank and maybe play with him a little bit—get him tensed up maybe and wondering what the hell was going on, get off alone and see how he handled himself.

Son left the highway at the county road pointing to Broke-Leg Creek, held back to see the Ford coupe make the turn after him, then was sure he was going to be followed wherever he went. That was fine with Son. He drove past the road that led up through the hollow to his place, went about two miles past it and turned off on a road that skirted the edge of an old worn-out pasture and led back into the woods, narrowing in the dimness and looking more like a trail than a road. His dad had used this road sometimes to haul in his corn and sugar, but it had not been used much in the past few years. Weeds grew tall down the spine of the road and brush closed in on both sides to scrape against the body of the pickup truck. Maybe Frank would be irritated, getting his car all scratched up. That, too, was fine with Son. He hoped to get Frank Long irritated.

Finally the road climbed up through dogwood and yellow pine and came out into the sunlight on the ridge that looked down over the Martin property: the pasture and the barn and sheds and the gray-weathered house, little squares way, way down below. Son's pickup bumped along in low gear, passing the place where Mr. Baylor had waited with his deputies the evening before, following the ridge trail through trees and clearings, until Son decided this was about far enough back and away from everything. He got out of the pickup and stood squinting in the sunlight, waiting only a couple of minutes before the Ford coupe came bumping along and pulled up next to him.

Frank Long's elbow stuck out the window. He said, "Well, here we are."

Son nodded. "Here we are." He watched Frank open the door and come stiffly out of the car and then press his hands against the small of his back and arch his body as he looked out over the land.

"It's a nice view," Long said. "But it don't compare to that cozy little setup you got back of town. That I'd say was about it for a Sunday afternoon—truck hid in a shed, jar of moonshine in the kitchen. Where was you, Son? I peered in, I didn't see nobody stirring anywhere. You all must have been down in the cellar putting up preserves." Frank Long grinned. "You helping that nice lady with her canning?"

Son grinned with him. "You aren't any little sneak, are you? You're a big tall skinny sneak. Grown man peeks in windows—what else you like to watch, Frank?"

"Being a little sneaky is part of my job, so I know what boys like you are up to."

"I'll tell you, Frank, anything you want to know."

"Anything?"

"Maybe just about anything."

"How's she, any good?" Long waited when Son didn't answer. "Well, is she? How many times you put it to her?"

Son kept watching him. Thinking, two steps, two and a half, fake with the right and come in with the left wide, hard against that bony nose and mouth, right where the hatbrim shadow cuts him. But Son knew he would have to keep going and finish it because if he didn't, the .45 would come out of the shoulder sling and he didn't know for sure what Frank had in mind, so Son held on. He didn't smile,

58

he didn't go stone-faced either. He just looked at Frank, telling him he had better ask real questions if he wanted answers.

"All I wondered," Long said, "was if she's the local whore or Son Martin's special stuff. All right, now I know, we can get to other things."

"Like whiskey," Son said.

Long nodded. "Like whiskey."

"Come on." Son walked out of the clearing into the trees and scrub, Frank Long catching up to stay close behind him.

Frank wasn't worried; he had lived in the mountains most of his life. He knew the dank smell of the forest and the feeling of silence in the tree dimness—silence, though there were sounds all around them, high up in the trees and in the dense laurel thicket. The sound of their own steps in the leaves, the sharp brittle sound of twigs snapping. He could follow Son anywhere and he could keep up and keep his sense of direction in the thicket and if Son figured to lose him in here, Son had something to learn. Hell, he'd traveled these paths. They were just barely trails leading into where they hid the stills. A man could tramp these woods till he dropped of old age, but if he didn't know what to look for he'd have to be dumb lucky to find anything. Water, that was what to look for: cool stream water a stiller had to have in order to run whiskey. In this hollow it would be Broke-Leg Creek and if Son was going to show him anything he'd have to take him to the creek.

Son showed him a rock house up in the limestone where his dad had once operated a still: more of an open ledge than a cave, with water seeping in and staining the rock a copper color. He showed Frank Long the aqueduct system his dad had made: split logs hollowed into troughs and laid end to end a quarter of a mile from the spring to the outdoor still. That was another one his dad had used. The third one was in the house Son had built the year he got married, and that still was operating today.

"Where's the house?" Long was following Son through the laurel, speaking to the back of the man's tan shirt.

As they came out of the thicket, Son pointed and said, "Down there in the trees. You see the roof and the smoke. I guess Aaron's got the fire going."

"Where you and your bride lived, huh?"

"For a year, before I went in the Army."

"Was she from around here? Somebody you knew awhile?"

"From Corbin. I knew her a few years. Then we seemed to get married all of a sudden."

"I know how that is," Frank grinned.

"Elizabeth never had any children, which I guess is a good thing."

He could picture her; he could see the dark-haired girl with freckles, a strong and healthy-looking girl, who had never been sick in her life until the influenza came to Marlett and spread up into the hollows. Son did not see her in the casket. He got home from Camp

60

Taylor the morning of the funeral and went directly to the funeral home where everyone was standing around waiting for him, and the undertaker was wishing they would hurry and get done with expressing their sorrow, because he needed this parlor for somebody else. So they buried Elizabeth Hartley Martin, 1898-1919, in the churchyard. Son got on the train to Camp Taylor and was back in Marlett seven days later for his mother's funeral and burial in the cemetery, next to his wife.

Son could picture her, the twenty-year-old girl he had married, but he seldom thought of her as his wife; he could see her smile and her nice even white teeth with the freckles across her nose, a pretty girl he had taken to dances and out riding in a buggy. He didn't think of her as his wife and it gave him a start sometimes when he remembered he had once been married. He would probably marry again. It seemed natural, though it wasn't a simple thing to do now—with Frank Long standing with his hands in his pocket squinting down the slope at the little house where Son Martin worked his still. Son watched. He said, "You want to look at the still?"

Frank Long turned, looking past Son, up the slope and to the dark ridges beyond. "Well, as you know, I'm more interested in old whiskey than new stuff. I'm interested to know where an old man would hide a hundred and fifty barrels." His gaze roamed over the slope studying the thickets and trees and the outcroppings of sandstone.

"Where'd the old man dig his coal at?"

"All over here," Son answered.

"I see where there might be some shafts. He worked all alone?"

"Usually. Sometimes Aaron helped him when he wasn't working the farm."

Long nodded. "The old man dug coal, Aaron farmed, and the both of them made whiskey. What I want to know, was the old man digging for coal or digging hiding places?"

Son was working a cigarette out of the packet in his shirt pocket. "There's only one way to find that out, isn't there? Go look in all the holes you come across, peer in and poke around and see what you find."

"That would take me some time, wouldn't it?"

"I don't know. Twenty years."

"Less I had some help."

"You think they can spare the men? I understand you Prohibition people are awful busy."

"I was thinking," Long said, "of getting people around here to help me, like the Blackwells and the Worthmans. I mentioned to Mr. Baylor this morning it might be the way to do it."

Son drew on his cigarette. "What'd Mr. Baylor say to that?"

"He said he'd like to be there when I ask them"

"I would too."

"Then I told Mr. Baylor I wasn't going to ask them. I was going to tell them."

"I see. Just order them."

"That's right. I say to them, 'You go out and find me Son Martin's hundred and fifty barrels. Find it or get him to tell where it's at, I don't care which. Because if you don't I'm going to start busting your stills one at a time, and I'm going to put all you boys out of business.' "

"Now you're telling me."

"Yes, now I'm telling you. Mr. Baylor said they need their stills to make a living and without the stills their families would go hungry and said something about the kids getting rickets and scurvy. You believe that?"

Son nodded. "They rely on their stills, that's the truth, with the good farmland washed into the creeks and river. I don't know anything about what would happen to the kids."

"But without money to buy food it would seem those folks would go hungry," Long said.

"It would seem so," Son agreed.

"So, what are you going to do about it?"

Son looked at him, drawing on his cigarette. "I don't see as it's my problem."

"You don't care what happens to them?"

"I think the Blackwell boys and the others are big enough to take care of themselves."

"After I put them out of business?"

"If you can do it. You haven't showed anybody how big you are yet."

"How about when they see their stills in little pieces?" Long was working in gradually, keeping his gaze on Son now. "They see their equipment shot full of holes and all busted to hell and they see the smoke still curling up from your cooker. What do they think then? The Prohibition man hits them where they live, but he don't lay a goddamn finger on his friend Son Martin. How do you think that will set with them?"

"I think you got to bust a still first," Son answered. "And I think you got to have more than that army automatic hid under your coat."

"But let's say I can do it."

"Frank, we'll be here. Show us something."

"I just want you to realize what's going to happen."

"If I don't tell you where the whiskey is."

"That's right. It's in your hands," Long said. "I promise you, if you don't do the right thing your neighbors are going to come down on you like a herd of bulls."

"Frank, you should have stayed in the Army where you got somebody to think for you. You start using your own head it's likely to get blown off."

"You keep thinking I'm alone."

"All I see is you."

"And all I got to do is call Frankfort and you'll see more Prohibition agents than you can count. I'm offering the easy way, Son, because we soldiered together and were buddies. But if you want me to be mean about it then boy you got trouble."

"Because we were buddies," Son said. "I appreciate that. Listen, because we were buddies I'll do you a favor, Frank, I'll give you an ax and let you go down there and chop up my still and pour out any whiskey you find. You write a report and say you found only one still in Broke-Leg County and you busted hell out of it and your boss says, Frank, you did a dandy job, now we'll send you some place else. Then you go there, wherever they send you, forget all about any hundred and fifty barrels a drunk soldier told you about. Figure it was drunk talk and go about your business and maybe you'll live to enjoy old age."

Frank Long grinned, shaking his head. "It is surely good to be talking to an old buddy again. Yes, I'm certainly glad I came here. Son, I'm not going to bust your still. I told you why. But I wouldn't mind taking a look at it—see where the best moonshine in the county comes from."

"Down there in the house." Son nodded toward the roof showing in the trees below.

"How do I get to it?"

"Path over there, through the bushes."

"Show me."

Son had dropped his cigarette stub. He paused now to fish another out of his pocket and light it. "Go ahead, I'm right behind you."

Long moved through the brush and stopped at the edge of a dry wash that came down from the slope above and dropped down steeply a good hundred feet to Son Martin's, where the bank of the wash had been lined and built up with stones, diverting the course of the gully away from the house. Frank Long looked down the open trough. It looked dry or crusted over; you couldn't tell about it this time of the year. He looked over his shoulder at Son coming up behind him.

"Is this all right?"

"That's the quick way, Frank. You can take it or go on over aways and find a switch-back trail the ladies use to go down."

"I asked you if it's all right."

"Well, it looks all right to me."

Long would have to agree to that, but he didn't know when it had rained last and he didn't know if the wash was dry or only covered with a thin dry crust. He stepped down off the bank, took another step and one more before his foot went through the crust. Long hopped as his foot sank into the mud, but with the next step his shoe disappeared and as he struggled to pull his foot out and keep his balance he went down, breaking through the thin dusty crust. He tried to get up and slipped again and rolled over to get his arms out and his hands in front of him, but he was going down the gully head first now, plowing open the thin crust, clawing at the mud, and taking chunks of it with him. Long had no chance against the month of spring rain that had seeped into the red dirt and turned the gully into a mud chute. He gave up, letting himself slide and roll until he came to a stop a hundred feet below, where the bank turned and was reinforced with stones.

He sat there a minute before pulling himself up, his clothes and one side of his face painted with the red muck. Long was still wearing his hat. He took it off, looked at it, put it on again, and stared up the wash, way up to where Son Martin stood waiting.

"A man has to be careful around here, Frank. Watch his step and know what he's doing. He'll find he can't rely on anybody's word." Son didn't raise his voice; his words carried clearly to Long, who unbuttoned his coat and drew the big .45 automatic, looking at it and then at Son as he held the gun in front of him.

"You want to get rough," Long said, "I can end this game right now."

"Maybe," Son said, "but not without getting the back of your head messed up. Put it away, Frank."

Long hesitated. Son wasn't going to trick him from a hundred feet away. He looked over his shoulder, hesitated, then slid the automatic back into its holster. Aaron covered him from the porch of the house, holding a 12-gauge aimed right at his head.

By Monday noon the story around Marlett was that Son had thrown Frank Long down the mud wash after Long pulled a gun on him. Aaron told it correctly at the Sweet Jesus Savior prayer meeting Sunday night; but it was natural for the story to take on weight in Son's favor. Son causing him to fall wasn't enough; Long deserved to be pushed. Lowell Holbrook told how Frank Long had given him the muddy suit of clothes and instructed him to throw it away—there was so much wet mud stuck to it, the suit would have to dry out for a week and then be beaten with a stick for another week. Lowell Holbrook said the suit was in a trash barrel back of the hotel if anybody wanted to see it. A few of Lowell's friends went to take a look.

By the time Frank Long appeared on the street that Monday, he was being referred to as The Hog Man, a nasty creature that liked to wallow around in wet clay mud. No one was sure who had made up the name though later Bud Blackwell claimed he said it first. Maybe he did. It was Bud Blackwell who said it to Frank Long's face.

Bud and his brother Raymond, and Virgil Worthman were standing at the corner down from the hotel entrance, probably waiting for Long, when he came out and walked right up to them.

Long took them by surprise. He spoke first, asking if Mr. Baylor had talked to them.

"About what?" Virgil Worthman said.

"If you have to ask then he didn't," Long said, "so I'll tell you myself."

"I don't know," Bud Blackwell said, "if we should be seen talking to you. They say you tell a person by the people he hangs out with."

"You won't have to talk," Long said. "Just get the wax out of your ears and listen."

Bud Blackwell glanced at his brother. He said, "Hey, you know who this is? Somebody must have hosed him off, because this here is The Hog Man."

Frank Long hit him in the mouth. Bud might not have gone down, but the curb tripped him and he fell hard in the street. He got up wiping his hands on his thighs; his right hand slid around to his back pocket and came out with a bone-handle clasp knife that he put to his mouth to pull the blade out with his teeth.

"Open it," Long said, "and I'll shoot you dead for assaulting a federal officer. You can come at me, boy, but if you use the blade or these others horn in, then out comes Sweetheart." Long patted the hard bulk of the automatic beneath his coat.

One thing about Bud Blackwell, whether it was to be knives or guns or a fist fight, he didn't stand around talking about it. He threw the knife underhand to his brother Raymond and went for Frank Long, who was waiting with his big bony fists and his reach advantage. He jabbed Bud hard in the mouth with his left and slammed the right into Bud's cheekbone; he took a couple of Bud's wild swings on his shoulder and forearm and waded in again with the jabs and hammered Bud's bloody mouth with the right and held up from throwing it again as Bud went down on the sidewalk and this time didn't get up.

Frank Long waited for Bud's brother Raymond and Virgil Worthman to look at Bud— both of them stooping over him—then gave them time to look up at him and make up their minds whether they were going to take a turn or pick up Bud and go home. Evidently they weren't having any, Long decided, because they didn't say a word or make a move.

"When that boy wakes up," Long said, "take him over to see Mr. Baylor and you all listen to what he says. I've done enough talking for a while."

Long had come out to take a walk and look over the main drag and maybe stop in a cafe for his noon dinner. But he changed his mind now and went back to the hotel, up to 205. There was no sense in fooling around, he had decided in the past few minutes. If these hardcase boys were going to gang him, it was going to take more than conversation to make them think in the light of reason. He was going to have to bust a few heads as well as stills. In his room Frank Long took off his hat and suit coat and laid the .45 automatic on the night stand as he sat on the bed. He lighted a thin cigar and picked up the telephone. Those smart-aleck boys wanted a fight, Jesus, he'd order up more fighting than they could stomach. When the operator came in, Long gave her the number of the federal Prohibition director in Frankfort. The operator took his name and room number and said she'd call him back and he hung up the receiver. Long waited.

They'd be surprised to hear from him, since he was supposed to be on a leave of absence. He'd told them he was needed at home because of sickness in the family.

When the operator called back she said the circuits were busy but that she would keep trying.

He said all right and hung up again. When the operator did get through to Frankfort probably the line would be busy. Then, it wouldn't be busy, but the phone would ring for about an hour before anybody in the office decided to answer it. Then the fat woman clerk would get on and he'd tell her who he wanted and she'd say he was out and didn't know when he'd be back. He'd give another name and the fat woman clerk would sound put-out as she said, all right, just a minute, and another hour would go by while the fat woman clerk stood over the water cooler talking to another woman clerk and the phone receiver lay on the desk, off the hook. He sure didn't enjoy waiting or taking crap like that from women who thought they were the cat's ass. There hadn't been any women clerks in the Army, but Jesus there had been enough waiting. The Army was famous for it: hurrying a man up and then making wait. Though it hadn't been a bad life, even with the low pay and usually lousy food and having to wear leggings and thick-soled shoes. In his life Frank Long had farmed, worked for a mine company, gone through the ninth grade of school, had served twelve years in the U.S. Army, Infantry and then Engineers. He had made sergeant and had a pretty nice room of his own in the barracks, but they never let him go to Officer's Candidate School and get a chance at the soft life. Hell, he'd probably be in today if they'd made him an officer. He didn't have anything against the service, but when someone told him they were looking for federal Prohibition agents it sounded good. You wore a regular suit and the pay wasn't bad; you were given a badge and a gun. Long wasn't sure what the gun would be, so he swiped a BAR he liked and took it along with him when he was discharged.

The old man, Mr. Baylor, had asked him, "What do you get out of this? A five-dollar-a-month raise?" Probably he wouldn't even get that. He'd put in his expense sheet and get a hard time from the fat woman clerk who would act like it was her money she was giving out.

The other way, keeping the whiskey himself—the minimum he stood to make would be forty-five hundred gallons times five dollars a gallon. Or, at the bootlegger's price of five dollars a fifth he could make over a hundred thousand bucks.

Hell yes, he had thought about it. He'd thought about it most of the time the last couple of days: find the whiskey, get somebody who knew what he was doing to ship the stuff out by truck to Louisville, and split the profit with him: some bootlegger who knew the market and ways to get to it. Long had a file on some pretty good boys. Some wanted, some in jail, some just released. One in particular Long couldn't get out of his mind, the perfect guy for a deal like this one, somebody who had the knowledge and experience to sell the whiskey and, at the same time, somebody who could be trusted. Hell, the man had been a dentist before becoming a bootlegger. You had to be pretty upstanding as well as smart to be a dentist.

Dr. Emmett Taulbee was his name.

Long got a two-ring binder out of his suitcase and sat down on the bed again as he opened it, flipping through pages of reports and "wanted" sheets until he recognized Dr. Taulbee's photographs, in profile and head-on.

There he was: Emmett C. Taulbee, D.D.S. Age fifty-one, a slight smile curling his lip and showing some of his upper front teeth. He must have thought they were something to show, though they protruded a little and were big horse teeth. Taulbee considered himself a ladies' man, and maybe there was some indication of that in the way he combed his wavy hair and let it dip down across one side of his forehead. He was also said to be a dude—wore expensive striped suits and detachable white collars on a blue shirt. His last known place of residence, Louisville, Kentucky. There was an address and a phone number, the typewritten phone number crossed out and another number written above it in pencil.

The photographs had been taken seven years ago, at the time of Dr. Taulbee's arrest for sexually assaulting a woman patient in his dentist chair.

At the trial the woman testified that she had been a patient of Dr. Taulbee's for several years.

No, he had not made advances or displayed an interest in her physically, not until she was in his chair for the extraction of her molar. She said Dr. Taulbee placed the mask over her nose and mouth and told her to inhale the gas slowly. She remembered the sound of breathing in the mask and the awful suffocating feeling for a moment. Then she was asleep. After that she remembered stirring and feeling a weight and something white over her, close to her face. She did not realize at first that it was Dr. Taulbee partly on top of her on the chair. She thought perhaps she was dreaming, until she felt something and moved her body and knew that her lower body was bare and that her legs were apart. When she screamed Dr. Taulbee twisted off her. He stood with his back to her for a moment, then hurriedly left the room. The woman testified that she found her undergarment on the footrest of the chair. Her skirt had been pushed up around her hips, but her stockings and shoes had not been removed.

She was an attractive woman in her early thirties, the mother of three children. In questioning her, Dr. Taulbee's defense counsel played with the implication that the woman had made up the story as a means of smearing Dr. Taulbee's name. Though they gave no reason why she would want to, nor did they accuse her of it directly. The woman answered all questions calmly, candidly looking at Dr. Taulbee from time to time to see how he was taking it.

Taulbee sat quietly most of the time. Occasionally he would smile or shake his head at the woman's testimony. His counsel did not put him on the witness stand, so the court did not hear from Dr. Taulbee. Though they did hear two additional women patients testify: one, that he had acted strangely and had touched her—held her arm or shoulder and had asked her if she was by any chance menstruating, because if she was the anesthetic might have an adverse effect on her. The other testified that upon leaving Taulbee's office after having had gas for an extraction, she felt her clothes disarranged, as if she had been sleeping in them or as if someone else had dressed her. Dr. Taulbee's license to practice was revoked and he was sentenced to one to three years in the State Penitentiary at Eddyville. While he was there his wife of twenty years divorced him.

Prison, Frank Long decided, was what changed the man's life. He met bootleggers and whiskey runners and evidently something about their business appealed to him. Dr. Taulbee was released after a year and was a good boy during the two years of his probation. Since then—during the past six years—Taulbee had been arrested four times for the possession of illegal alcohol, but had not been convicted even once. He was making money and sure had better lawyers than the one he had at the assault trial. Taulbee was a businessman with a working force and a good profitable operation that reached from Kentucky up into Ohio and over into Indiana and he would be just the one for a deal like this one. Hell, Taulbee was the only one Long knew of who could handle a hundred thousand dollars worth of grade-one whiskey.

He had met Taulbee twice, both times after raids on Taulbee's warehouses. The last time they had sat around the police station questioning Taulbee and waiting for his lawyer to come and Frank Long had got along pretty well with him. Taulbee didn't seem to be worried; he told some pretty good jokes and grinned when everybody laughed. Long liked a man who didn't let anything bother him. Sitting around there Taulbee gave everybody a cigar and said, well, now if somebody else could supply the whiskey and the girls, he'd as soon come to this jail as most of the speaks he did business with. He was honest, right out in the open, and they said he sure liked girls.

Long did not make a judgment about Dr. Taulbee's assault on the women. If he liked to do it to them while they were sleeping, that was his business, but Jesus, it was sure better when they were squirming around. It didn't seem enough to send a man to prison for. Those women had probably been asking for it anyway.

The more Long thought about it, the better it looked to him. Long and Taulbee, partners. One job, that was all. He wasn't about to turn criminal for life. One job and he'd take his cut and go to California or somewhere. Just one job and not do anything wrong ever again.

Before the phone rang Long picked up the

receiver and waited and then said to the operator, "Listen, never mind that call to Frankfort. I got a number in Louisville I want you to get me."

five

Dual Meaders told the filling station man ten gallons of ethyl and sat to wait, his elbow pointing out the window and his pale-looking eyes gazing straight ahead, half closed in the afternoon glare.

Behind him, in the back seat, Dr. Taulbee said, "Ask him where's a good place to eat."

The girl sitting with Dr. Taulbee, Miley Mitchell, a good looking eighteen-year-old girl with brown hair and nice dimples, said, "God, around here?"

"Ask him," Dr. Taulbee said.

Dual Meaders got out of the La Salle; he walked back to where the filling station man was holding the nozzle in the gas tank opening and asked where was a good place to eat.

"Right in front of your nose," the filling station man said, nodding across the highway to the white frame house with the FOUR STAR CAFE sign on a pole in front.

Dual Meaders didn't like the man's answer. If the man had been close enough to see Dual's light-colored eyes, he would have smiled or laughed or said something else to show he was just being friendly and not smart aleck at all. But he didn't see Dual's eyes and Dual didn't have time, at the moment, to show them to the man. He opened the rear door and said, "Across the street."

Dr. Taulbee squinted at the FOUR STAR, frowning, showing his front teeth. "Ask how far to Marlett."

"I know how far," Dual said. "Corbin's another fifteen miles, Marlett's sixty, seventy more."

"We could wait till we get to Corbin," the girl, Miley Mitchell, said.

"Not the way my stomach's growling," Dr. Taulbee said.

Miley was studying the cafe. There were no cars parked in front. "I don't know. It's after three, maybe they're not serving now."

"Honey," Dr. Taulbee said, "get out of the car, will you?"

Holding the door open, Dual was looking at the filling station man who was watching the gauge on the gas pump. It still burned him the way the man had answered. Dumb hick saying right in front of your nose. Dumb hick pumping gas in his filthy dirty overalls.

At the edge of the road Dr. Taulbee looked around and said, "What're you waiting for?" Dual closed the car door and followed after them.

As he was crossing the road, the filling station man called out, "Hey, what about your car?"

Dual kept going. Over his shoulder he said, "Leave it where it's at."

The man called out something else, but Dual didn't pay any attention. Jesus, it was hot in the country already, a spring day, but like the middle of August. He headed for the shade of the cafe, opening the door that Dr. Taulbee, a few steps ahead of him, had let close.

The place was empty: counter, tables, and booths all empty. A radio was playing in the kitchen and there was the sound of voices, but no one appeared until they were seated at a booth.

The woman who came out of the kitchen looked them over as she stood at the counter and filled three glasses of ice water from a pitcher, then smiled as Dr. Taulbee gave her a pleasant nod. From the city, the woman decided, judging by their suits and striped ties, the older one with a rounded stiff collar and a tiepin, but they seemed friendly. Probably father and son, or uncle and nephew—they looked enough alike to be related though the older ones hair was nice and wavy and the younger one's was slicked straight back and shiny. The woman didn't know about the girl. She could be the daughter of one or the wife of the other. Though the woman had a feeling the girl wasn't related to either of them. The girl was certainly pretty, a little thing but with a pair of grown woman's ninnies; if they were her own and not a pair of socks balled up inside her undies. They were travelers on the road, maybe going to visit kin or to attend a wedding or a funeral. It was too early in the year for them to be on a vacation.

They drank their ice water and asked for Coca-Colas and when the woman came back with the Cokes they ordered from the top of the menu, talking among themselves as they told her what they wanted: the older man ordering salmon croquettes and the salad and asking the younger one about Marlett and how far out from town was a certain place—"the Caswell place"—which sounded like somebody's farm. They made the woman wait talking about Marlett, but she didn't mind because then she would learn something about them. The woman looked at the girl for her order, but it was the one with the slick shiny straight hair who spoke up and told her he'd have the barbecue beef and two orders of fried potatoes; though he was so thin and pale, with sunken cheeks, he didn't look like he'd ever eaten a full dinner. He had a toothpick in the corner of his mouth he must have picked up at the cashier's counter coming in. He rolled the toothpick to the other side of his mouth and said, don't worry, Caswell would have enough room for anybody they brought. The young girl said she guessed she'd have the salmon croquettes also; but the Four Star Cafe woman was listening to the older one say they would learn soon enough if they needed the extra room or not and when they got there they'd stay at the hotel if the burg had a hotel. The younger man said if he remembered correctly it was called the Cumberland Hotel, and the young girl said again she would have the salmon croquettes, if the woman wouldn't mind, and another Coca-Cola. The woman had never been to Marlett, though she knew where it was and was pretty sure there was no tourist attractions over there like natural caves or mineral springs. With them mentioning this Caswell place, or whatever the name was, the woman was pretty sure they were going to visit friends or kin.

It was a little while after she had served them their dinner and was back with more bread and butter for the skinny slick-haired one that the young couple came in. They sat at a table after standing at the cashier's counter and looking around the empty restaurant for a while.

As she put the bread down the skinny one said, "Dog, I like that tan suit that boy's got on."

The woman went to the counter to pour two ice waters and studied the new couple as she took the waters to their table: nice looking, both of them in their mid- or late-twenties with city written all over them. They were trying to appear at ease, but the woman could tell they were self-conscious and knew the three people in the booth were looking at them. Yes, they sure were: the skinny one was looking this way and then laughed out and the young girl with the pretty dimples giggled and the wavy-haired man was grinning, showing his teeth. The young couple ordered ham sandwiches on whole wheat and iced tea. When the woman told them they didn't have any whole wheat the young man said white would be fine.

The Four Star woman took their orders to the kitchen. She was at the counter fixing their iced tea when the skinny slick-haired one from the booth walked over to the young couple. She heard him say something about the man's suit. The man looked surprised and said, "Well, thank you."

"Where'd you get it?" Dual asked him.

"I believe it was in Cincinnati," the young man said, fumbling with the button of his suit coat to open it.

As he did, pressing his chin to his chest to look at the label, his wife said, "Where else?" She opened her eyes wide and laughed brightly to show she was at ease. "You just bought it about a month ago."

"I like that kind of material," Dual said. "It's not as woolly or hot as some suits."

"Thank you,"

"It's gabardine," his wife said.

Dual frowned, cocking his head as he studied the light tan double-breasted suit. "How much you pay for a suit like that?"

"This suit?" The young man trying to act natural, looked at the label again, as if the price tag might be there. "I think it was about fifty bucks."

"Forty-four," his wife said, "I remember because you wondered if you should spend that much."

"Forty-four dollars," Dual said, nodding, still appraising the suit. "Okay, I'll buy it off you."

The young man grinned, going along with

the joke. "Gee, if I had another one I would, I mean I'd sell it to you."

"I don't want another one," Dual said. "I want that one you got on."

As his wife laughed, letting Dual know she had a good sense of humor, the young man laughed and kept smiling as he said, "What am I supposed to do, take it off right here and give it to you?"

Dual wasn't laughing; he wasn't smiling either. He said, "That's right." He pulled his wallet out of his back pocket, looked inside closely as he fingered the bills, and dropped two twenties and a five on the table. "You owe me a dollar," he said.

The young man let his smile fade, then smiled again with an effort, shaking his head and looking beyond Dual Meaders now toward Dr. Taulbee and Miley Mitchell. Raising his voice to a pleasant tone he said, "Is your friend serious?"

Dr. Taulbee took a bite of salmon croquette and rested his fork momentarily on the edge of his plate. "He's serious. If there's one thing you can say about him, he's serious."

"But you can't just come in and tell a person you want to buy his clothes—" The young man was appealing to Dr. Taulbee. "You just don't do it."

"You wouldn't think so," Dr. Taulbee said, buttering a slice of bread and folding it in half to take a bite.

Miley glanced over at the table and went back to her salmon croquettes. They were pretty good; a lot better than she thought they would be.

"I can't take off my suit. Right here."

"Why can't you?" Dual asked him.

"I mean why should I? You can't just come in here and take anything you want."

"I'm paying for the suit, ain't I?"

"But I don't want to sell it!"

"Mister, do you believe I care what you want? Take off the suit yourself so I won't have to do it and maybe tear it," Dual said.

The young man's wife wasn't laughing now. She seemed afraid to move and her face was white. She said in a low voice, but loud enough for Dual to hear, "Urban, call the police. Ask the lady to call."

The Four Star woman was watching from behind the counter, holding the two iced teas. The young man looked at her now, a glimmer of hope in his expression. He said, "Are you going to stand for this going on in your place? You allow anybody to come in here and threaten your customers?"

"I work here," the woman said. "I don't own it or anything. The owner is Mr. James C. Baxter, but he ain't here right now."

The young man's wife said, "Well, will you please call the police?"

"I don't know—" The woman stood rigid holding the iced teas. "I don't know what's going on here. I don't know if it's a joke or what."

"He's threatening my husband!"

"Well, I don't know what he's doing. I was to call, I wouldn't know what to tell them."

"Ruth," the young man said, "never mind. Let's forget it. Let's just leave. Are you ready?" He was keeping his voice low and controlled, doing a fair job of acting natural.

Dual Meaders let the young man push his chair back and stand up before he reached inside his coat and came out with a .38 revolver. The gun looked heavy in Dual's slender hand; his wrist bent with the weight of it so that the barrel pointed low on the young man.

"I'll put a hole in your suit," Dual said, "if you don't start taking it off.

The young man opened his mouth, but not to speak. The gun barrel and Dual's expression held him wordless. He couldn't believe this was happening; except that the skinny, pale-looking fellow was pointing a gun at him and it was the realest thing he had ever seen in his life. He didn't want to look at his wife. He was afraid she might say the wrong thing and make the fellow mad. The fellow seemed calm, even patient, but that was it, he was too calm: his face was like a dead man's face with the eyes open, a skeleton man who was too small to wear the suit in the first place. It wouldn't even fit him. If he asked the fellow to try it on he'd see for himself. But if the fellow took it wrong, thought he was calling him a squirt, God, there was no telling what he might do. That's why the young man from Cincinnati looked straight ahead and took off his coat without saying a word.

When he hesitated, Dual said, "Now the pants. Hey, what size shoe you wear?"

"Nine B."

"Too big. Keep your shoes and them garters. Jesus Christ, I don't want no garters. The tie's all right. I'll take that and you don't have to pay me the dollar change." Then, studying the young man as he undressed, Dual said, "Take everything off, right down to your skin."

"What?"

"Come on, take off the drawers and the undershirt."

The young man pleaded, "There's no need. You don't want my *under*wear," and forced himself to smile.

"Please—" his wife said.

Dual's eyes moved to the woman. "Don't you like to look at him with no clothes on?"

"Please," she said again. "Take the suit and let us go."

Now Dual's eyes shifted to the young man. "You better step out of those drawers, mister."

Dr. Taulbee used a doubled piece of bread to push the last of his salmon croquettes onto the fork. He glanced over at the young man, then at Miley, and put the salmon in his mouth. "You're not looking," he said.

Miley's head turned to study the young man, briefly. "What's there to look at?" She was eating her salad, wiping the side of the bowl with a piece of bread. "They don't have enough mayonnaise in the dressing," she said.

"Do you like that outfit she's wearing?"

"Who?"

86

"The guy's wife."

Miley looked over at the couple again. "It's all right. I don't wear much brown."

"It might look good on you."

Miley shrugged. "Maybe. I think it's too small though."

Dr. Taulbee straightened in the booth, raising his head. "Dual," he said, "we'll take that dress too."

The young man's wife stared and hesitated as long as she could and said, oh please, and finally began to cry. Her husband put his hand on her shoulder and pulled down the zipper in back and helped her off with the dress.

"Pink teddies," Dr. Taulbee said. "I like teddies on a shapely woman."

"She's not much," Miley said.

"Well, we don't know for sure."

Dr. Taulbee straightened again. "Dual, we might as well see the whole show."

The woman pleaded until Dual turned the revolver on her and her husband again patted her shoulder and stood close to her. The woman pulled the straps from her shoulders, peeling the silk undergarment down and stepped out.

Miley was finishing her salad. "I told you," she said.

"No, they're not too bad."

"Are we going to have dessert?"

Dr. Taulbee continued to stare at the woman. "Ten, twelve pounds she'd be all right."

"I wouldn't mind ice cream or pudding," Miley said.

Dr. Taulbee touched his mouth with his napkin. "I think we'd better get along." He looked over at the Four Star woman holding the glasses of iced tea. "Miss, if you'll bring us a check please." Dr. Taulbee got up; starting for the door he paused to look at the couple standing naked by their table, the woman huddled close to her husband and sobbing. "Honey," Dr. Taulbee said, "there's nothing to be ashamed of. I've seen women get by just fine with a whole lot less than you got."

Dual paid the check. By the time he was outside with the suit over his arm, squinting in the sun glare and waiting for a truck to pass before he could cross the highway, Dr. Taulbee and Miley had reached the La Salle and were getting in. The car had been moved from the canopy of the filling station and stood off to the side in the hot sun. Another car was next to the line of three pumps and the filling station man was standing with one foot on the car's rear fender, holding the gasoline hose—the same one that had said to Dual Meaders, "right in front of your nose."

Dual approached the first pump, at the front fender of the car. He didn't pay any attention to the filling station man, though he noticed the guy in the driver's seat of the car watching him—an old guy, a farmer. Dual took out his pocketknife and slashed it through the pump hose as the guy watched. Then he gave the guy a look and walked off toward the La Salle. Dr. Taulbee would get sore if he had to wait too long.

Dual Meaders gave himself the gabardine suit as a birthday present. He turned twenty-five the day he drove Dr. Taulbee and Miley from Louisville across the state to Marlett. Dual had never been over in this hill country before. He was originally from Memphis, Tennessee; had left home when he was fourteen and had been back only once since—and then by accident, because some hobos had robbed him and thrown him off the freight as it was passing through Memphis. That's what he had intended to do, pass through, but they pushed him out of the boxcar near Chickasaw Gardens and he picked cinders out of his face and hands for a week. (There were still spots on the heels of his hands where the gravel had been ground into the skin.)

Not long after that, when he was eighteen years old, Dual was charged and convicted in Kentucky of assault with the intent to commit bodily harm, after he had poured gasoline on a sleeping hobo and set him afire.

Dual had thought this was pretty funny and had even cracked a smile in the courtroom when the prosecuting attorney described to the jury the old man running down the street screaming. The old man lived, though he spent two months in the hospital. Good—Dual didn't have any use for hobos since the time he was robbed and thrown off the freight train and he admitted he was out to get them. What he got was three years in Eddyville and Dr. Taulbee as a cellmate during the last year of his sentence. They got along all right. Dual liked Dr. Taulbee because even though the man was educated and a dentist he did not act biggety or think he was better than anybody else. He didn't act tough and he wasn't a fighter, but if a con got mean with him, Dr. Taulbee could usually quiet the man by talking to him. Only once did a con cause him real trouble. The con told him he wanted a sack of tobacco and cigarette paper every day or else he'd break Dr. Taulbee's arms, both of them. Dr. Taulbee gave the man what he wanted until Dual got the tin knife made in the metal shop and, on a rainy afternoon in the yard when a bunch of them were huddled in a doorway, slipped the tin knife into the con's side. Dr. Taulbee didn't have any trouble from then on. After he was released from Eddyville he wrote to Dual and told him to look him up. Five months later Dual was out, working for the doctor and having one hell of a good time.

Boy, things happened fast; and it seemed everything had a reason. If he hadn't been sent to Eddyville, he'd never have met Dr. Taulbee. If he hadn't been thrown off the freight train and got them cinders in his hands, he wouldn't have poured gasoline on the bum and lit him up. Hell, and if he hadn't been riding the rails, he wouldn't have been thrown off. Take it back all the way. If he hadn't killed that boy with the rock, he wouldn't have run away from home. (The fat son of a bitch was way bigger than he was and had been picking on him and beating him up all during the school year. So one day coming home Dual had got up on the garage roof with the rock that must have weighed twenty-five pounds and, when the fat boy came along the alley, Dual dropped it on his head.) So if he hadn't dropped the rock, he wouldn't be working for Dr. Taulbee.

He sure liked working for him. It was a good easy job with plenty of excitement and all the booze and babes he wanted. What he liked especially was the .38 Smith & Wesson. God it felt good holstered there under his arm: blue steel and a hard hickory grip and with it he could do just about anything he wanted. It was sure better than a heavy rock or a wavy tin knife.

Dual said to the rearview mirror, "This Frank Long is supposed to be at the hotel?"

As Dr. Taulbee looked up Miley stirred, her head resting against his shoulder, her eyes closed. "That's what he said."

"Marlett ain't very far now." Now Dual's eyes were on the uneven blacktop beyond the dark dusty oval hood of the La Salle. "The Caswell place is supposed to be up back of town. He said turn at the cemetery and keep going, you can't miss it, a two-story house, was painted white one time."

"You told me," Dr. Taulbee said, sitting patiently and looking out at the rolling green countryside.

"You remember Caswell at Eddyville?"

91

"The name more than the face."

"Boyd Caswell. It was something, I remembered him being from Marlett. You said we're going to Marlett, I thought of Boyd Caswell right away. You know what he said when I called him?"

"I think you told me that also," Dr. Taulbee said.

"He said, 'Jesus H. Christ, come on. There ain't nobody here but me and my old daddy and he's half deaf and full blind.' "

"We'll see how blind he is," Dr. Taulbee said. Dual looked up at the rearview mirror. "Caz says it, it's a fact."

"You said he was in for armed robbery?"

"Sure, but me and him was friends. I mean if you can't trust Caz, you can't trust anybody."

"Now you're talking," Dr. Taulbee said. "Say that every night before you go to bed."

"What I was wondering—if we shouldn't stay there awhile, get the lay of the land before we see this Frank Long."

Dual held his gaze on the road and the voice behind him said, "No, we'll talk to Long first. We want to see whether he's real or wasting our time."

"Or setting a trap."

"Or that," Dr. Taulbee agreed.

"How do you tell?"

"You don't. You get something on him."

"What if he's playing square?"

"You still get something on him."

"I don't know." Dual shook his head. "I don't believe I remember this one."

"I remember him," Dr. Taulbee said. "I remember two different times meeting that boy and both times thinking to myself, If you went looking to buy yourself a Prohibition agent you'd find this boy sitting on the counter."

"He never came to you before this?"

"No, not till his telephone call the other day."

"It could still be a trap he's setting for us to walk into."

"Don't forget it either," Dr. Taulbee said. "Let's think about it in silence so this little girl can get her rest."

Dual straightened up to look at Dr. Taulbee in the mirror. "She sleeping?" Miley was cuddled against him with his arm around her now.

"Like a baby," Dr. Taulbee said. "Bless her heart."

A few minutes later Dual Meaders said, "You are now entering Marlett, Kentucky. Population two thousand one hundred and thirty-two."

Lowell Holbrook came down the stairs to the lobby and went right to the desk, where Mrs. Lyons was closing the register and putting it on the shelf under the counter.

He said, "I was sure the girl was with the younger guy; I mean I thought she was his wife. But she had me put her bag in the same room with the older guy." Lowell was frowning, looking at Mrs. Lyons for an explanation. "Is that her father?"

93

"Her husband," Kay Lyons said. "Dr. and Mrs. Emmett Taulbee, from Louisville."

She began going through a stack of mail that must have come in, Lowell decided, while he was upstairs. He said, "Well, the other one can't be her son."

"Mr. Dual Meaders, also from Louisville."

"They staying long?"

"They didn't say."

"Well, the younger guy's in 208 and the married ones are in 210. Is that right?"

"That's fine, Lowell."

"Mrs. Lyons? The older one, upstairs, he asked me what room Frank Long was in."

Kay looked up from the letters, holding one in hand. After a moment she said, "Then he must be a friend of theirs."

"Don't you think it's funny?"

"No, I don't think so," Kay Lyons said. "Why?"

"Well, coming in and asking for a Prohibition agent."

"He could still be a friend."

"I suppose," Lowell said. Though all afternoon he kept thinking about them: seeing the man with the big toothy smile and the girl looking out the window and the younger one with a tan suit over his arm, like he was going to send it out to have it cleaned, though he never did. He would think about them and wonder if he should tell Mr. Baylor.

And Mr. Baylor would say, "These birds checked in and asked for Frank Long. Well, now what do you want me to do, put them in jail?"

94

That was it, what they done outside of asking for somebody? Frank Long was a Prohibition agent, but he was also a person, with kin anyway, even though he might not have any friends.

So Lowell didn't tell Mr. Baylor about them. He told himself if Mrs. Lyons wasn't going to worry, he wasn't either. Hell, tomorrow they'd probably be gone and he'd never see them again.

Lowell found out that was wrong the next morning—when he saw the three of them walking through the lobby and out the front door with Frank Long. He watched them get into a big car that looked like a La Salle and drive away.

six

Son could hear the dogs down in the hollow, far below through the stillness of the trees, the clear, sharp racket of the foxhounds onto something. Son stood on the porch, at the edge of the morning shade, looking out across the yard to where the road came up out of the hollow. Aaron came around from the side of the house and both of them stood listening for a minute.

When he was sure he had located the sound of the dogs in his mind and could picture them bounding out of the thicket and coming this way, Son looked over at Aaron.

"There isn't any rabbit would run up the road, is there?"

"No rabbit I know of," Aaron said. "They chasing a car."

"Whose car they say it is?"

The Negro cocked his head. "They don't say whose, only it's a car."

"I guess one. They're both right together."

Aaron nodded, looking at Son now. "Jes' one, but maybe full of dudes. You want me to go down a ways?"

"No, go on up to the still. Hey, Aaron? With a shotgun."

Aaron came up on the porch, as tall as Son and heavier through the chest and shoulders. "Maybe it jes' a friend come for breakfas'," he said.

"I didn't invite anybody." Son waited while Aaron went inside and came out with the Remington 12-gauge "Aaron," he said, "somebody comes in and wants to knock the still all to hell, let them do it."

"I'll be nice."

"But if somebody shoots at you or you think they're about to, don't hold back."

"No, sir, I let them make the intentions known."

"They can have the still if they want it."

"Tha's right."

"But they can't have us."

Aaron grinned. "Tha's right."

Son sat down on the top step to wait. He got up and went into the house and came out wearing a dark hat with a funneled brim that

he pulled down close to his eyes—the way
Frank Long wore his hat—and looked off at
Aaron crossing a hump of the meadow, heading
for the slope and the house up in the trees. Son
sat down on the step again.

This is where he was when the La Salle
came up out of the hollow with the foxhounds
yipping, leading the way. Son didn't recognize
the car, so he didn't get up. He didn't move.
He sat with his arms on his raised knees and
his hands hanging limp. He watched Frank
Long open the front door on side and get
out.

He watched the driver in the tan suit come
around the front of the car. Son had to look
at that suit again, wondering why the man didn't
wear a smaller size, so he wouldn't have to roll
up the cuffs of his pants like that.

He watched the dude and the good-looking
young girl get out of the other side and come
around the back of the car: the dude wearing
a straw hat cocked to the side and a brown
striped suit that was snug around his heavy chest
and stomach, the dude looking like he should
be carrying a sample case of jewelry or ladies
underwear. Next to him Frank Long looked
like a skinny old-time Baptist preacher.

Son watched the four of them gather to
stand looking up at him, Frank Long two
paces in front, the spokesman. Well, he could
talk if he wanted, though Son knew already who
was in charge of the party. He had a fairly good
idea about the boy in the tan suit also and wasn't
fooled by the suit being too big for him. The

only one he couldn't figure out was the girl, who stared right up at him and didn't look away when he shifted his gaze toward her. There was a bold little thing. Maybe not so little either. Son didn't nod or speak because it wasn't up to him, it was up to Frank Long.

Frank said, "I might as well introduce my associates here and get to it, seeing how you're so busy. This here is Dr. Taulbee, he's a scientific whiskey expert who's come to sample your supply for the government and give it a grade and tell whether it's any good or not. This little lady is Miss Miley Mitchell, who is Dr. Taulbee's expert assistant and secretary, you might say. And here you have Mr. Dual Meaders, come here as a special investigator to help us capture your daddy's whiskey, if you force us to do it that way. And folks," Frank said then, looking up the stairs, "this is Son Martin, my old army buddy."

Son still didn't move. From the top step he could see them all and didn't have to turn his head to study any one of them.

"Son," Frank went on, standing relaxed, with his suit coat open and his thumbs hooked in his vest pockets, "Dr. Taulbee here has a proposition I think you're going to like. See, I got to thinking, why start a lot of shooting and trouble when maybe there's a simple legal way to settle this. Your daddy went to a lot of work to run a hundred and fifty barrels and maybe you, as his heir, are entitled to something for it, even though you're breaking the law by having it. As you know, possessing is as much against the law as making." Frank waited.

But Son didn't give him any encouragement.

"How's that sound to you? A proposition."

Dr. Taulbee shifted his weight and shook his head and moved up next to Frank Long to put his hand on Long's shoulder and give him a friendly shove. Grinning in the morning sunlight Dr. Taulbee said, "Frank, you old horse, you're doing as much good as a one-legged man in an ass-kicking contest. You ask how it sounds, you haven't *told* him anything."

"I'm getting to it," Long said, standing straight now, serious.

"Well, you sure take a while." Dr. Taulbee looked up at Son Martin, giving his honest-to-God, good old-boy smile. "Don't he though? We could be out here till suppertime before he'd have it told, I swear." The down-home drawl rolled out naturally and Dr. Taulbee moved in closer to plant a polished shoe on the bottom step.

The girl had her hands on her hips and was moving about idly, a step this way and that, looking down at stones and kicking at them lazily with the pointed toe of her pumps, then looking up and squinting in the sunlight and brushing her dark hair from her forehead. She wasn't dressed for being out here; she wore a skirt and jacket and pearls and little earrings. She was really pretty. Son decided she was pretty enough to be an actress or a singer. While the one in the tan suit kept looking up at the porch, nowhere else. He wasn't dressed for being here either, but he didn't look like any actor or singer. Or like a federal man or a special investigator. He didn't change his expression or seem to be aware of the heat or the sun glare or the dust that would blow across the yard when the wind came up. He kept his eyes raised to the porch.

"My," Dr. Taulbee said, "but it's getting warm. I wonder if you would have a cold drink of water in the house."

"Water's over there." Son nodded toward the pump standing in the yard, a few feet from the corner of the house.

"Well, friend, if you'll let me have a cup then."

"Cup's on the pump handle."

"Yeah, I see it now," Dr. Taulbee said, maintaining, with an effort, his friendly down-home tone. "Miley, be a nice girl and fetch the old doctor a cup of spring water, if you will please."

Miley stared at him a moment before walking over to the pump.

Dr. Taulbee kept his friendly gaze on Son. "What I was thinking, if we could go inside, out of the heat, I'd like to tell you about this proposition Frank mentioned. I guarantee you'll be interested."

"I don't think so," Son said.

"Well, you'll want to hear it before you say yes or no for sure, won't you?"

Son shook his head.

Dr. Taulbee held on. "My friend, that doesn't make any sense. A man comes to you with a deal, you want to at least have the courtesy to listen to it, especially if it's going to save you a lot of trouble and maybe even your life. You understand what I mean?"

"There's no deal," Son answered. "No chance.

Dr. Taulbee's easy expression vanished. "Mister, you get tough with me, I'll tear your goddamn scrub farm apart and if I don't find what I want, I'll hang you from that porch beam—you hear me?"

A smile touched the corners of Son's mouth as he stared at the man. They looked at each other and got to know each other without a word being spoken. It wasn't a long moment in the silence between them, but it was there and it was enough. The squeaking, air-sucking noise of the pump handle broke the silence.

Miley called over, "I can't get this thing to work."

"Forget it," Dr. Taulbee said.

"I haven't pumped water since I was a little girl."

"I told you forget it!"

Frank Long shifted his position, impatient now. He said, "Son, listen to us, all right? I guarantee you'll want to think on what we tell you."

"Is it your idea," Son asked "or this scientific whiskey expert's?"

"Both of us together thought of it."

"Frank, you showed us a badge when you

marched in here." Son looked over at Dr. Taulbee. "I want to see the paper that says he's a scientific whiskey expert."

"There ain't no paper says he is."

"Then get off my place."

"Son, I'm telling you that's what he is, hired by the U.S. Government."

"Or hired by you?"

"Son, you're getting into things that don't matter when all we want to do is lay this deal on you."

Dr. Taulbee said, "Dual, if you're tired of standing with your finger in your nose, look for where a man would hide a hundred and fifty barrels of shine."

"I been thinking about it," Dual said.

"Now wait a minute," Frank Long said. "He's going to listen to us. Aren't you, Son?"

"If you say it and leave," Son answered.

"Dual," Dr. Taulbee said, "do you take that kind of talk?"

"Not since I can remember. No, sir, I didn't ever take it from any east Kentuck farm hick."

"If he talks like that again, what're you going to do?"

"I could shoot his ears off."

"Show him your gun, Dual."

"Right here." Dual pulled the .38 out of his suit coat and pointed it at Son's face. "You see it, mister?"

Son didn't say anything.

"I asked if you see it."

"You better answer," Dr. Taulbee said.

Son nodded. "All right. I see it."

"There," Dr. Taulbee said. "He's going to be a good boy now and he wants us to go into the house and have some coffee and a nice talk. He's saying, 'Yes, sir, Dr. Taulbee, I certainly want to listen to your deal 'cause, god-*damn*, I get my ears shot off I won't be able to listen to anything.' Isn't that what you're saying, boy?" Dr. Taulbee was grinning, his old self again.

"Come on," Frank Long said.

Dr. Taulbee looked at Miley who was sitting on the board cover of the pump well. "Honey, you'll make us some coffee, won't you?"

Dual shifted his position for the first time. He said, "I don't want any. I'm going to start looking around."

Dr. Taulbee reached over to slap him on the shoulder. "If that's what you want to do, you go ahead."

"It's what I come for," Dual said. "Seein's I'm the special investigator."

The way Dual Meaders had it figured, the one hundred and fifty barrels were hidden somewhere close to Son Martin's house. The stuff had been out of sight for eight years, though during that time people had been roaming all over the Martins' land playing find the whiskey. Most of them would have stayed up in the hills looking for two reasons. Because they'd be afraid Son would catch them if they got too close to his house. And because the old man had dug coal up in the hills and a mine shaft was the logical place to hide that much stuff—if it was all in one place. Dual wasn't sure about that. It could be spread all over.

Where he'd like to start looking was right in the house. While they were talking he'd kept studying the house, the way it was built against the side of the hill with its high front porch. Under the house itself was a cellar—and a stone wall of that cellar could be covering an old mine entrance that burrowed straight into the hill, which wouldn't be a bad place to hide it; where you could live on top of it and know the second anybody came looking and got warm.

When they had all gone up the steps and into the house, Dual squatted down to look under the porch. There was no need to duck under; he could see there was no opening in the stone foundation—hunks of limestone chunked together with mortar. So Dual walked around, past the pump, to the side of the house.

There it was, the wooden door to the cellar angled against the base of the house. The door creaked on rusty hinges as he lifted it, then pushed it over to let it bang hard against the ground as sunlight filled the stairwell and formed a square of light on the floor of the cellar. Going down inside Dual had a kitchen match in his hand ready to strike, but there was enough natural light to show him everything there was to see: shelves of quart and half-gallon fruit jars, shelves of jars from floor to ceiling, cases of jars, and jars lined on the shelves and filmed with dust. All of them empty, waiting to be filled with moonshine.

He didn't find any corn meal or sugar—they must have kept that at the still. He felt along the stone wall that would be against the hillside and didn't find any loose stones to indicate an opening: which shot his idea of the stuff being buried under the house.

But he did find something that surprised him: a new looking Delco Farm Electrification System, the motor-generator and the row of glass batteries taking up half of one wall. Looking it over, Dual was thinking it was an expensive outfit to light up an old farmhouse that one man lived in. He felt along the wall and traced the wire going up through the ceiling to the room directly above him. Well, maybe this Son Martin was ascared of the dark and liked plenty of light. Dual grinned at the idea. He wished he could grin like Dr. Taulbee, showing teeth like big square pearls, but his own teeth were crooked and tobacco stained and he didn't much like seeing them himself. He had brushed them every day the first couple of months he worked for Dr. Taulbee, but the brushing didn't make them any whiter, so he had quit.

There wasn't anything else down here.

There wasn't much out in the barn either. Walking inside Dual could tell this wasn't the place: a back-country barn that wasn't much bigger than a two-story house, weathered and starting to fall apart; like the owner didn't plan to be here long. The floor was hard-packed dirt; no boards might be covering a big hole underneath. A stack of baled hay filled a corner of the buildings. Something could be behind or under it, but Dual wasn't going to go pitching hay bales around with his new gabardine suit on. Some other time. There was nothing here in the dirty smelly place but the hay and some grain sacks, empty stalls and stiff harnesses and hackamores hanging from pegs. Up the ladder was half a loft. Stepping back to one side of the barn Dual could see there was nothing up there. Out the window were two mules in the yard, nuzzling the ground, penned in there by a split-rail fence that looked like they could knock over if they wanted to. Christ, get this job done and get back to Louisville where things were going on, that was the ticket. Dual never did care much for farms; there wasn't anything to do.

He had spotted the roof showing way up on the slope in the trees. As they drove into the yard Frank Long had said that's where the still was, in a house Son Martin used to live in.

So Dual Meaders trudged up there from the barn—a long walk in the open sunlight, the dusty pasture steeper than it looked—feeling the muscle-pull in his thighs and sweating under his new suit like a goddamn field hand before he reached the trees.

Dual noticed the grave over a couple hundred feet from where he stood: the grave and the post and the little fence, close to a steep rocky section of the slope. He studied on it a minute before saying to himself, "It's a funny place for a grave with a light post, but you ain't going to get a hunnert and fifty thirty-gallon barrels in a six-foot hole," This Son Martin was a spooky gink with his goddamn lights everywhere.

By the time Dual had made his way up through the pines and brush and had clawed through the tangled laurel, losing the path about every time he turned around, he had his new suit coat open and was wiping dusty sweat from his forehead and out of his eyes. Woods might look cool and fresh from a distance, but he didn't like any part of them. In the trees and thickets, with hardly any breeze seeping through, it was close and steamy and, Christ, there was an awful sour rotten smell hanging over the place. Dual located the source of the smell: over to one side of the little house, where they had cleaned out their mash barrels and left the fermented grain to rot. Christ, there would have to be some awful drunk snakes and lizards around here.

The house looked like it was about to fall off its stone foundations that leveled the porch at the two front corners. There wasn't much of a slope here in this clearing; it was like a bench on the slope, with pines and stone outcrops towering way above. Dual looked at the two windows and the wide open door and the smoke wisping out of the chimney pipe: not much smoke, probably burning dogwood or beech. Two barrels of mash stood by the door. Dual glanced at them as he stepped up on the porch and went inside, expecting somebody to be here because of the smoke, but the still was working all by itself.

It was about as clean and orderly a still as he'd ever seen, a first-class copper outfit you could take a picture of and say under it here's how to do it, boys: fifty-gallon capacity cooker with a low fire burning in the grate and a gleaming copper gooseneck coming out of the cap to carry the steam over into the flake stand: an open barrel filled with limestone spring water, water so clear Dual could see the worm of copper that was fitted to the gooseneck and coiled down through the fifty-gallon barrel. Inside the coil the steam was right now being cooled by water and condensed into the clear moonshine whiskey that dropped from the spigot into a half-gallon jar.

About six gallons a day they'd draw, Dual decided. He preferred aged amber-colored whiskey every time, but this stuff didn't look bad, probably because the place was so clean.

He stopped outside on the porch and looked over the small clearing, then noticed again the two barrels of mash by the door and bent over the nearest one. A crust that looked like dried mud covered the fermentation taking place inside the barrel.

"When the cap falls that mash is ready to run."

Dual came around with his revolver out of his coat and put it square on Aaron standing with the shotgun across the crook of his arm, standing a few yards away in the clearing that had been empty a moment before.

"You put your ear close on the barrel,"

Aaron said, "it sound like meat afryin'. Few mo' days we pour off the beer and cook it."

Dual said, "Boy, lay that shotgun down."

Aaron grinned; lazy, slow-moving, head-shaking nigger, he seemed barely to shift his stance, but in the movement he came around enough so that the double barrels on the Remington, angled across his arm, were pointing directly at the man on the porch.

"You want something in my house?" Aaron asked him.

"You're pointing that at me, boy."

"No, suh, it pointing out of my arm."

"I'm telling you you're pointing it at me." Dual held the revolver in front of him and hadn't moved. "No nigger points a gun at me, boy."

"Mister, I ain't pointing the gun, it pointing itself."

"Put it down."

"I like to, but my finger is caught in the trigger. I'm afraid to move it."

"I'll plug you right between the eyes, nigger. You see that?"

"Yes, suh."

"You want me to do it?"

"No, suh, cuz if you do, I'm afraid this old shotgun will fire off and blow them mash barrels all to hell and anything standing close to them."

Dual Meaders had never felt such a terrible sharp urge in him. He felt if he didn't fire, if he didn't squeeze his wet hand on the grip and keep squeezing it, he'd rush the nigger and tear him apart with his fingernails. But the twin barrels of the shotgun, the round black 12-gauge holes, were as real as the terrible urge and they held him, like a wild animal caught in a headlight beam, and saved his life.

It was not worth dying to kill a nigger. Not when there could be another time to do it. Any time he wanted. Let the nigger think about that for a while.

"No," Dual said, "I don't want anything in your house. But I'm going to come back again sometime. I expect you know that."

Aaron nodded. "I expect I do."

Dual holstered the .38 and rebuttoned his coat, lingering there, waiting for the nigger to make a mistake. Finally he stepped off the porch and walked past him into the thicket. He felt all right now, calm and himself again, but Christ, that nigger was going to pay for getting him worked up like that. He couldn't believe it, the nigger standing there holding the gun on him. Christ, what was the world coming to?

Son punched two holes in a Pet Milk can and set it on the table. He and Frank Long took some, but Dr. Taulbee and the girl drank their coffee black. Son took a sip of his as the girl watched him. It was weak and about all he could say for it, it was hot, but he nodded to the girl and gave her a little smile. She'd worked on the coffee like she was preparing a full dinner.

Son didn't push or ask questions; it was still

their party. But nobody seemed ready to get to the point until the coffee was on the table. Then Dr. Taulbee sipped his and said, "Ahh—" and blew on it close to his mouth and sipped at it again.

Frank Long bit off the end of a cigar and said, "Goddamn-it," and picked shreds of tobacco from his tongue. "The proposition is this."

As he paused then to light the cigar, Dr. Taulbee said, "The proposition is we buy the whiskey from you."

"Who's we?" Son asked.

"We. *Us.* The United States Government."

"I didn't know the government was in the business."

"Not in the business. But there is such a thing as government spirits. Didn't you know that? For various reasons, like medicinal use, and so on." Dr. Taulbee leaned in close to the table, his eyebrows raising. "Now, somebody has to be making what the government approves and buys, would you agree to that?"

"Whiskey don't make itself," Son answered. "I'll agree that much."

"Fine." Dr. Taulbee grinned. "We're starting to get along, aren't we?"

"Who pays me for the whiskey?"

"The government does."

"How much?"

"A fair price. You tell us what you want and you submit it like a bid contract through Frank here's office. Of course there's one thing." Dr. Taulbee waited for Son to jump up and say what, but Son just looked at him and Dr. Taulbee had to continue. "You have to pay a government tax on what you've produced, otherwise it's illegal whiskey." Dr. Taulbee sipped his coffee and eyed Son over the rim. "First though, of course, I'd have to taste the whiskey before issuing a stamp."

"Buy it," Son said, "you can taste all you want."

Dr. Taulbee sat back and laughed. "My goodness, do you think the government is dumb? They aren't going to buy anything unless I tell them it tastes good."

"Then they don't buy it," Son said.

Frank Long bit down on his cigar, hunching in and said, "Jesus Christ, who do you think you are holding up the goddamn United States Government?"

Son shifted his gaze to Long. "Frank, if you want to buy it, give me the money and I'll tell you where it is and get out of your way. Otherwise you're just blowing smoke out your ears."

"All right," Dr. Taulbee said, "now let's discuss this like gentlemen. I believe we're getting somewhere and there's no need to get excited, is there? Son here has a product for sale and we're the customers. Right? Now like on any deal it's a matter of the two parties getting together. Maybe there's a little give and take, but finally it's worked out to everybody's mutual satisfaction. Miley, honey, you want to pour a little more? That coffee just hits the old spot, doesn't it, boys?"

Son glanced over at Miley. He wasn't sure

if she was still looking at him, or looking at him again.

She said, "Who cooks for you?"

"I do," Son answered. "Or Aaron. Whoever wants to."

"You aren't married?"

"Miley,"—Dr Taulbee's tone was pleasant but loud—"I said we'd like some more coffee—"

She got up to go to the stove. "It isn't very good, is it?"

Son watched her move, too slowly for a young girl; she stood with her back to them.

And Dr. Taulbee was saying, "Supply and demand is the golden rule of commerce, boys. When somebody has something other people want, then by golly he gets paid for it. Son, how much do you want?"

"Twenty-seven thousand dollars."

Frank Long started laughing, forcing it and shaking his head. He said, "Now who do you think's going to pay you twenty-seven thousand dollars for a hundred and fifty barrels of moonshine?"

"If you're not, Frank, we can talk about foxhounds or the price of corn or you can get the hell out of here and I won't mention it again."

"Now, wait a minute," Dr. Taulbee said. "The man says that's his price. All right, you got to start somewhere in working out this supply and demand business." He waited while Miley poured the coffee, then stirred his thoughtfully, though there was no sugar or cream in the cup.

"I was just thinking," he said. "If the government can't pay your price—I mean if they believe it's too high and just won't budge on it—what would you say if I was to offer to buy it as a private citizen?"

Son placed his spoon in his saucer. "I'd say you were a bootlegger."

Dr. Taulbee laughed now, curling his mouth and showing his big teeth. "Whoeee, my goodness, if the folks in Frankfort heard you say something like that. What I mean, if I bought it as a speculator, paid you for it, but kept it right where it's at, gambling on repeal coming about during the next year or so. If the country stays dry, I lose my shirt. But if the Eighteenth is repealed—and I'll admit I got a hunch it's going to be someday—I buy me some tax stamps and market the booze before the big distillers get going again. Even with repeal it's chancy; somebody could under sell me and I'd end up drinking it all myself." Dr. Taulbee grinned his finest grin. "But if it's all as good as you say it is, then having to drink it might not be so bad either. Son, what do you say?"

He said, "What does this Prohibition agent think about it?"

"Frank's a reasonable man. Aren't you, Frank? If you believe like I do that repeal's coming, then it would be wasteful to pour off a hundred and fifty barrels of good stuff, wouldn't it?"

Son watched Frank Long pretend to consider this and nod thoughtfully.

"I guess it would be a waste at that," Long said.

Now it was Son's turn to nod. "Well, then," he said solemnly, "if you feel that way, Frank, I guess I'll just keep the whiskey myself and wait on this repeal you all are talking about."

Neither Frank Long nor Dr. Taulbee was smiling. They sat quietly for a minute staring at Son Martin. For what it was worth Long said, "You can't afford to speculate, Son, but he can. That's the difference. That's why I could permit him to keep the whiskey, but not you. I mean I wouldn't let you take the chance."

Son didn't bother to reply and Long, in the silence that followed, added nothing to the statement. Dr. Taulbee was the thoughtful one now and he was not pretending or stalling or getting ready to present a new proposal. He was accepting reality, resigning himself to the fact that Son Martin was not going to be talked out of his whiskey. It was going to take work; no doubt a pretty dirty kind of work.

Dr. Taulbee was glad to see Dual Meaders coming up the steps. There he was, the sweet boy, coming right when he was needed, marching in on cue, looking hot and tired and meaner than usual, which was all right with Dr. Taulbee. Yes, *sir*, when in doubt turn Dual loose, and the meaner he felt, the better. Dr. Taulbee got up from the table.

"Boy" he said mildly to Son, "I see you're going to make us work, which Frank claimed right along would happen. I'm not opposed to work, but I am a little disappointed in you, at your hard-headed stupidity, because we're

115

going to get your whiskey and I think you must know that, whether we have to break your legs to get you to tell or put you under and find it ourselves."

Son shook his head. "If I don't tell, you won't find it."

"Just a minute, boy. I'm not finished my speech. We're going to let you have a few days to think about it and watch the trouble start to come down on you, then we're going to come back and ask you again in a nice way, 'Son, where's the whiskey at?' I'll bet you ten dollars right now you tell us. If you don't tell, you win the bet and I'll put the ten spot in your pocket when we bury you."

Son waited a moment. "Is that the end of the speech?"

"All I'm going to say," Dr. Taulbee answered.

"Then I'll see you in a few days."

Son waited on the porch as they walked toward the car. He had better not say anything else. He had better hold on and, when they were gone, get up to the still and see if Aaron was all right. He was looking that way, toward the hillside and the faint trail of smoke above the roof, when Dr. Taulbee called to him.

"One more thing, Sonny."

Son looked over.

"Dual here showed you his gun, but he never showed you what he can do with it."

Son waited. Let him talk; don't say anything.

"See that barn yonder? See the two mules in the pen? Watch."

Dual drew his revolver, standing in front of

116

the car with one foot on the bumper, a good thirty yards from the split-rail fence at the side of the barn. He didn't hesitate. He raised the .38 and fired and fired again and one of the mules jerked its head up and sidestepped and, as its knees buckled, fell heavily to the ground.

Dual looked over at Son on the porch, the revolver still in his hand. Dr. Taulbee looked over and waved good-by.

Frank Long rested his arm on the top of the seat cushion and shifted around to look at Dr. Taulbee in the back seat.

"He'll tell once we get done with his neighbors."

Dr. Taulbee's head moved with the motion of the automobile and he seemed to be nodding. "It might work."

"I'll guarantee it. If you can get the men."

"All we'll need."

"I think about eight anyway. You can get eight?"

"Dual," Dr. Taulbee said, "call when we get back to the hotel."

Dual looked up at the mirror. "Then I'll go out to Caswell's and see they have a place to stay."

"You're way ahead of me, aren't you, boy?"

Dual smiled with his mouth closed, his eyes on the road. He didn't know what to say to that.

Miley sat close to the side window, staring at the fence posts and telephone poles and thickets and empty fields.

117

She said, "Why doesn't he just run?"

Dr. Taulbee's head drifted up and down. "Who?"

"If he knows he might get killed, why doesn't he just give you the whiskey? Or run away and forget it?"

"You sweet little thing," Dr. Taulbee said. "Because he's dumb."

"I can't understand that. He seems smart to me." Miley was silent, picturing seeing him smile as he raised his coffee cup. "How come he's not married?"

"His wife's dead."

"When did she die?"

"I don't know. A long time ago."

"He never got married again?"

Dr. Taulbee was looking out the window.

"I'd think some Marlett girl would have got him before this." Miley was silent again. He was nice looking and owned land. Why wouldn't he just get married and forget about the whiskey? She said, "What does he expect to get out of it?"

"Pain," Dr. Taulbee said, "if he thinks a minute. And anguish."

"I can't understand him—"

"Sweetie, don't worry your pretty head."

"Why he'd risk getting killed for nothing."

"Some people are funny," Dr. Taulbee said.

Miley was turned to him with a serious expression. "Why don't you buy it from him?"

"Because we don't have to."

"You offered to buy it at first."

"Sweet thing, if he didn't believe it, why do you?"

"I thought you meant it."

"We were trying to get him to tell," Dr. Taulbee said, "without trying too hard."

"Maybe he would sell it to you though."

"Except now we're not buying," Dr. Taulbee showed his teeth. "Sugartit, why don't you just sit back and enjoy the ride."

Miley sat back. It seemed like they were always driving somewhere, always in the car looking at the same wire fences and telephone poles and plowed fields, always the same run-down farm houses and the same filling stations at the crossroads, the same MAIL POUCH and NEHI signs and the same skinny old men in overalls looking up as the car passed.

It was hot in the car. Miley rolled the window down as far as it would go. She didn't care if the wind blew her hair. She was going back to the Hotel Cumberland, Room 210, and if the doctor was in the mood he'd have her hair all messed up anyway in five minutes, his too, with his waves down on his forehead or sticking out on the sides. She'd smell his tonic and the breath sweetener he used, sweet little things like bird shot he was always popping in his mouth. He had clean habits, but, God, his stomach was a size and after he was through doing it—all the while whispering dirty little sweet things in her ear—he would rest on top of her for a couple of minutes, sprawled out like a giant seal lying on a rock.

She had to wait till he stirred and finally rolled off before she could go into the bathroom. When she came out, he'd be lying on his back with his eyes closed and his mouth open, the round white mound of his belly rising and falling in peaceful sleep. Miley would put on a kimono and maybe read a magazine, waiting to see if he wanted to do it again when he woke up.

Sometimes she wished she was still working in the house. If there were no customers or, like in the afternoon when usually only one or two would come by, the girls would sit around talking and laughing or she and another girl would go shopping and have lunch out. It wasn't ever boring. It was usually fun, and interesting to meet new customers, to see a group sitting in the parlor and wonder which one was going to pick her first. It was nice to get a good-looking young one, though some of the old boys, like Dr. Taulbee, fooled you and had little tricks the young studs hadn't learned yet. She hadn't met any man who was so ugly that he repulsed her, and only once in a while did she get one who was smelly or whose breath was so bad it was hard to smile at him. The clientele was mostly a higher class, who could afford clean habits and ten dollars a trick.

Dr. Taulbee had got in touch with her after the house in Louisville was closed by the police. Dr. Taulbee had been a customer of hers for almost a year; she liked him and she appreciated him taking care of her now. He was generous and it was a pretty interesting and exciting life. Even the automobile trips to different places weren't too boring. The only thing that bothered her about the arrangement was the feeling, lately, that she was being wasted. God, Dr. Taulbee was the only man she had gone to bed with in the past five months. It seemed a shame with all the nice-looking fellows around. Dual Meaders didn't interest her—ugh, he'd be quick and serious and never say a word or crack a smile; get up, get dressed, and go. But she had been wondering, since meeting Frank Long and knowing he was in 205, what he would be like. And now she found herself picturing Son Martin taking his shirt off and looking at her and smiling. He probably wouldn't say much but—Miley made a little bet with herself—he would be something to experience.

Dual let them out in front of the hotel. Going up the steps, Dr. Taulbee gave her a little pat on the fanny and said, as if he had just thought of it, "Hey, honey, I know what let's do before dinner."

Miley smiled and Dr. Taulbee winked at her, running his arm around her waist.

"He didn't have to shoot the mule," Aaron said. "What would he want to shoot a mule for?"

"He likes to shoot his pistol," Son answered. He was harnessing the other mule. They'd drag the dead one out of the yard and bury it somewhere down in the hollow.

"I got a gun I like to shoot," Aaron said. "Next time I do it too."

Son shook his head. "No next time."

"He shoot a mule, the mule don't even know what the man want. I had him in front of me," Aaron said. "I could have shoot him for going in my house. I didn't know he was going to shoot no mule."

"Forget about him."

"He say he coming back, I don't forget about him."

Buckling the harness, Son paused. "He'll kill you if you're here. It's his business."

"I let him try."

"No, you go away for a while. You got family in Tennessee, haven't you? A sister? Visit her till this is over."

"I got two sisters and a old uncle. But I live here thirteen years."

"I know you have."

"Since the time you go in the Army and your daddy hire me to help him."

Son shook his head. "This has got nothing to do with you."

"They want the whiskey I help make."

"And if they think you know where it is, they'll ask you and break one of your legs and ask you again."

Aaron stared at him, his broad shoulders sloping and his arms hanging at his side. "You afraid I'd tell them?"

"I know you wouldn't," Son answered. "So they'd have to kill you."

"If they want to try," Aaron said. He brought

122

over a coil of rope to tie around the dead mule. "That's all the talking about it I'm going to do."

seven

Five days following Dr. Taulbee's visit, E.J. Royce drove up the hollow to tell Son about the raid on the Worthmans place:

How the dirty son of a bitches in their suits come in the dead of night without any warning and took all the moonshine they could carry off and tore up the still with axes and shot Uncle Jim Bob Worthman through the neck when he came outside with a shotgun that wasn't even loaded.

Mr. Baylor had sent E.J. with word that Son was to get over there, since it was Son's good old army buddy, Frank Long, who led the raid and Virgil Worthman would swear to it in court. Son said to E.J. Royce, what court? And E.J. said, he just wants you over there, probably because nobody knows what to do. Their still was gone, smashed to pieces, and Uncle Jim Bob, with a hole going in his neck and a big hole coming out, would probably never talk again, if he lived.

The Worthman place was less than two miles away in a straight line over the hills, but more than five miles through the hollows and around by road, On the way E.J. Royce told

Son everything he knew about the raid, which wasn't much. Mr. Baylor had sent him over just a few minutes after they got there. Other people were arriving, E.J. said, hearing about it and coming out. By the time they got to the Worthman farm the yard looked like a family reunion was taking place. There were a dozen cars and trucks in the yard and along the dirt road, a bunch of children climbing on one of the trucks. The grownups, mostly men, were standing around and staring at E.J. Royce's official car as it drove up. The men nodded or seemed to as Son got out and nodded to them, but nobody said anything. They stood with their grim serious expression and those that were in the yard, by the porch, stepped back so Son could walk up to the house and go inside.

He saw Kay Lyons first, who had probably not been out here since she was a little girl. She was helping her aunt, Mrs. Worthman, put cups and spoons and more sugar on the table where Mr. Worthman and Virgil and Mr. Stamper and Mr. Blackwell sat with Mr. Baylor. These men looked up, but it was Bud Blackwell, over against the wall in a rocking chair, his high-top shoes stretched out in front of him, who said hello to Son.

He said, "Well, Son, your old buddy was here last night." Bud was relaxed and seemed pleased with himself.

Son wasn't going to bother with Bud Blackwell right now. He kept his eyes on Mr. Worthman, in his overalls and old suitcoat and

124

top button of his shirt buttoned, who had lived here half a century and had made whiskey a quarter of a century and never in his life had realized trouble because of it. Mr. Worthman, staring at his cup as he stirred it, looked as if someone in his family had just passed away. Virgil Worthman had a cold mean look on his face, clenching and unclenching his jaw, that may have been the way he felt or may have been for the benefit of his friend Bud Blackwell, Son wasn't sure which.

"I seen him in the light," Virgil said. "There was no doubt as to who it was. They were carrying these high-powered flashlights. One of them said something to Frank Long; said, 'Frank—' and put a light on and that's when I seen his face, right there in the yard after Uncle Jim Bob had been shot. They didn't bother coming over to look at him. Well, I'll tell you, I'm going to look at Mr. Frank Long after I shoot him 'cause I'm going to make sure the son of a bitch is dead."

"Virgil," Mr. Baylor said, "kindly shut up and let your dad tell it. I want Son to hear this, and then I'll tell you what you're going to do and what you're not going to do."

Kay Lyons handed Son a cup of coffee. She came back with milk and poured it in herself, looking at Son's face as she lifted the pitcher away, but not saying a word or telling him anything with the look.

"We never did see their cars," Mr. Worthman said. "They left them down the road. We heard the cars when they drove away, after, but

125

not when they come. Some of them walked up to the house and the others went over across the crik to the still, knowing where to find it. It was a little washtub outfit we had setting deep in the trees but these people went right to it."

"So somebody knowing where the still was led them to it," Mr. Baylor stated, and there was silence in the room.

"They'd never found it in the dark," Mr. Worthman said, "without knowing where it was at."

Mr. Baylor was hunched over the table, his gleaming steel frame glasses holding on Mr. Worthman. "You heard them over there, did you?"

"We heard them. We heard some shots and we run outside. We don't know these other people are in the yard till Uncle Jim Bob come out with the shotgun. As he appeared somebody fired from the darkness, and Uncle Jim Bob made a sound like he was gargling and fell to the porch. After they was gone, we went over to the still and seen how they'd put bullet holes in the cooker, then taken axes and chopped up everything, the mash barrels, everything."

Mr. Baylor said, "They took some stuff you'd run?"

"Most of it. They broke some jars too. Didn't pour it out so we could use the jars again, broke them."

"Before they left, what was it the one said to you?"

"We were on the porch tending to Uncle Jim

Bob, this one calls out, 'Worthman, you listening?' I said, 'I hear you.' "

"Was it Frank Long's voice?"

"I don't know. I don't remember his voice any."

"What'd this voice say?"

"It said if I was to rebuild my still, they'd bust it again. They said they'd bust every still in this county if Son Martin didn't hand over his hunnert and fifty barrels."

Mr. Baylor waited, giving the silence time to settle. His steel frames gleamed as he looked from Mr. Worthman to Son and back again. "What'd you say to that?"

"I don't remember I said anything."

Stretched out in the rocking chair, Bud Blackwell said, "I'd a told the son of a bitch something."

Mr. Baylor turned on him, a skinny bird with its neck feathers ruffled. "Like you told Frank Long the other day on the street corner? I know all about how you told him," Mr. Baylor said. "If you're through telling then I'll tell you a few things."

Bud's dad, at the table across from Mr. Baylor, said, "Now wait a minute before you say too much." Mr. Blackwell had once been as smart-mouthed and sure of himself as Bud; he was an older, smaller version, now balding and wearing a Teddy Roosevelt mustache to make up for his bare expanse of forehead. "Long had a gun on Bud when he hit him."

"Is that right?" Mr. Baylor said. "Well, if you were there, then you saw your little sonny boy pull a bone-handle knife before he got his ears beat off."

"Who told you that?"

"Your other boy, Raymond. Now, if you're through I'm going to tell you how things are."

"They aren't going to sneak up on us," Bud Blackwell said. "You wait and see when they try it on us."

Every once in a while Mr. Baylor remembered his blood pressure and his seventy-three-year-old heart and would make himself breathe slowly with his mouth closed. To fall dead while beating Bud Blackwell with a pick handle wouldn't be too bad; but to go out screaming at him and slobbering and popping all the veins in his face would leave the memory of a mess they had to clean up before they put him in a box.

Mr. Baylor said to Bud, "What happens if you shoot a federal Prohibition officer?"

"They bury the son of a bitch," Bud grinned. "If'n they find him."

Mr. Baylor had breathed slowly in and out enough that he was still in control, a kindly and wise old man. He said, "Bud, honey, that's true. But you know what else happens? Whether they find him or not, you got the whole United States Government after you, because they know where that boy was going and who he was to see."

"A man comes at you with a gun," Mr. Blackwell said, "You by God better meet him with a gun."

"Is that a fact?" Mr. Baylor asked pleasantly.

"Man to man. He shoots at you, you shoot at him."

"If the man wants to keep his still," Mr. Blackwell said, "and isn't ascared to defend it."

"Fighting for hearth and home." Mr. Baylor nodded thoughtfully "That's a noble idea, but let me remind you of one thing. Stilling is against the law of this land, and if you're caught at it and resist, they got every right to shoot you full of holes. We have never had any federal people here before but, boys, we got them now. Aggravate them and they will stay till this county is wiped clean of stills."

"If I can't sell moonshine," Mr. Worthman said, "how'm I supposed to provide for my family and feed them babies playing in the yard?"

"How're you going to provide if you're dead?" Mr. Baylor asked him. "Or if they send you to Atlanta for five years? Listen, do you realize, as a county law officer I'm obliged to help these people?"

"Jesus," Bud Blackwell said, "with all the whiskey you drink?"

"I'm telling you what I'm supposed to do. I'm saying you got to quit stilling till they get tired of hunting and go home."

"They wasn't hunting when they come here," Mr. Worthman said. "They walked right to the still like they'd been to it before."

"That's another point," Mr. Baylor said. "If there's some person among us who's telling where the stills are, then it's all over, boys. You don't have a chance."

With his solemn expression Mr. Worthman said, "I can't believe a person would do that. Somebody around here who's bought whiskey from me. It would have to be somebody around here."

"That's the first thing we do," Virgil Worthman said, "find the one's helping them."

Mr. Baylor turned on him. "Do that, Virgil. Find him out of the hundred people you know by name who come here and the hundred you don't know. You never had any trouble before so you'd sell to anybody's got four dollars. Well, there's trouble now, boys, and you got no choice but to leave off stilling till they go home."

"Or move your stills."

Everybody in the room including the women by the stove, looked at Son Martin.

Arley Stamper, who had not spoken a word through this meeting, sitting next to Mr. Baylor, said, "Move them where?"

"Hide them," Son answered. "Your still's been sitting in the same place for ten years, with ruts and beaten paths leading to it. Now it's time to move the whole outfit and keep moving it every week if you feel the need."

Arley Stamper nodded, but Mr. Blackwell wasn't taking on any heavy work today. He said, "Move it where? How far you talking about?"

"Move it anywhere you want and cover your tracks," Son answered, "and don't tell anybody where it is. I mean don't even tell anybody here. Arrange some other place for delivery that isn't anywhere near the still."

"That sounds like pure nigger work, don't it?" Bud Blackwell said. "All that lifting and carrying and moving. Is that what you're going to do, Son?"

"If I decide to keep running."

Bud Blackwell shook his head like he was tired already. He said, "Hey, Son, 'stead of us doing all this moving and hiding, why don't you give them the hunnert and fifty barrels? That's all they want, ain't it?"

Right now if he had that pick handle, Mr. Baylor decided—in this quiet room with everybody staring at Son Martin—he would swing it at Bud Blackwell until he died of a stroke and went straight to heaven and would never hear what Son answered or stay around to see the end of this dirty business. But he didn't have that pick handle.

And he heard Son Martin say, "Bud, you tend to your whiskey business and I'll tend to mine."

Mrs. Lyons had hardly said a word since she got back from the Worthman place about one o'clock in the afternoon. She stayed in the office going through some figures—what looked like the same page of the ledger for quite a while—and it was like pulling teeth for Lowell Holbrook to get any information out of her.

"Well, what do you think's going to happen?"

"I don't know, Lowell."

"You think they'll hide their stills?"

"I haven't any idea."

"I mean didn't they say if they were going to or not?"

Then she would be concentrating on the figures and he would have to ask her again. He had to ask her three times was Son Martin there and what did he think of the situation? Finally she said yes he was there, but she didn't mention anything he said. Mrs. Lyons was acting funny. It was natural she would be worried; the Worthmans were kin and Uncle Jim Bob was her great-uncle or some such relation. But besides being worried she seemed to be acting funny, like something else was on her mind that had nothing to do with the Worthmans, or at least had not been mentioned.

A little before two o'clock Frank Long and Dr. Taulbee and his wife came down the stairs and went into the dining room. Lowell noticed the time. A pretty late dinner today.

He hadn't noticed Frank Long leaving the hotel the night before. Which didn't mean anything: he could have been on a room-service call or Frank Long could have been out all day. One thing Lowell was certain of, Dr. Taulbee and his wife hadn't gone anywhere. He'd taken some Coca-Colas and ice up to 210 just before going off duty and they had looked pretty settled: the doctor sitting up in bed smoking a cigar, reading the newspaper and his young wife standing by the window with a green silk-looking robe on brushing her hair.

The thing Lowell wondered about now: if Frank Long had been on that raid like they said,

132

had he taken that BAR rifle with him? Was it up there in 205 now? If it was, could a person look at it and tell if it had been fired?

Lowell watched the three of them come out of the dining room at twenty-five past two. It gave a funny feeling, thinking about the BAR rifle and seeing Frank Long. He expected them to go back upstairs, but they stood there a minute talking. Then Dr. Taulbee's wife turned to walk away, and Dr. Taulbee gave her a little pat on the butt. Lowell and Dr. Taulbee and Frank Long all watched her walk up the stairs with her fanny moving from side to side. Then the two men turned and walked out the front door.

If you think about it, Lowell said to himself, you won't do it.

He wasn't sure why he wanted to, except it was a scary thing to do and it would, somehow, put him in the middle of the excitement that was going on. Lowell tried not to think any more about it than that. He got the passkey on the brass ring from behind the desk and went up to 205, right to the door and opened it and, Jesus, there was the big suitcase laying on the bed.

You're here now and another minute won't make any difference, Lowell said to himself. Will it?

He didn't answer that yes or no; he went over to the suitcase and unbuckled it and opened it and there it was, the big heavy beauty of a gun, broken down and strapped in snug. Lowell lifted a two-ring binder out of the

133

suitcase so he could get a better look at the weapon, then leaned in close and sniffed it, getting a strong smell of oil in his nostrils. The gun certainly didn't look like it had been taken out and fired. Lowell wished it was put together so he could lift it in his bare hands and feel the weight of it. He looked at the binder in his hand—nothing written on the blue cover—and dropped it in the suitcase; then picked it up again and opened it. There were a few typewritten pages he didn't bother to read but, when he got to the pictures, his interest picked up and he started reading the men's names and descriptions and records of arrests and convictions. He was starting to skip through, just glancing at the pictures now, when he saw Dr. Taulbee's face looking up at him, grinning at him with those big white teeth.

Lord in heaven, Lowell said to himself, and started to read about Dr. Taulbee.

Frank Long turned at the Baptist Church and shifted into second gear as they started up the grade. Ahead, on the left side, he could see the stand of cedars and part of the small farmhouse showing. Frank waited until the car was almost to the front yard.

"That's where the woman from the hotel lives. Mrs. Lyons."

Next to Long, Dr. Taulbee turned enough to get a brief look at the house through the rear side window. "*Mrs.* Lyons, uh?"

"She's not married any more."

"Well, now, maybe I should be nicer to her."

Long glanced over at him. "What would you do with two women?"

"The same thing I do with one."

"I mean you got Miley along. Isn't she enough for you?"

"If you mean by enough, all you want," Dr. Taulbee said, "little Miley can dish it up. But she is one woman and Mrs. Lyons is another and, mister, they are all different. Each one has her own little pleasures and secret tender places. Each one is potentially the best one you ever had."

"There's the Caswell place up on the right."

Dr. Taulbee was looking at Frank Long. "You wouldn't mind a little bit of Miley, would you?"

"She's a good-looking girl."

"Well, Frank, maybe when I'm through with her. How'd that be?"

Long had a tight grip on the curved top of the steering wheel. Past the ridge of his knuckles he was looking at the farmhouse: at the vines climbing its walls, at the yard grown over with weeds and brush, and the sagging barn that was missing boards and part of its roof.

"I was saying—there's Caswell's."

Dr. Taulbee studied the place. "They ain't much for farming, are they?"

"Not a blind man and anybody drinks as much as Boyd does."

"You tell me," Dr. Taulbee said, "because

135

little Dual could be wrong about Boyd Caswell. Dual thinks anybody was at Eddyville is a first-class citizen."

"Boyd took us to Worthman's still last night," Long said. "I guess he's been there enough times he can find it drunk or sober."

Dr. Taulbee propped one hand against the dashboard as they turned into the yard. "Well he's in it now, isn't he?"

"The cars are in the barn if you're wondering." Long drove past the side of the house and pulled up in back as Dual Meaders came out the screen door in his shirt sleeves and shoulder holster, his hands deep in his pants' pockets.

"Bless his heart." Dr. Taulbee grinned and yelled out, "Hey, boy!"

Dual came over to the car and pulled a hand out of his pocket to open Dr. Taulbee's door, giving him his slight, closemouthed smile. "We're all in there waitin' on you," he said.

The old man at the kitchen table looked up with sightless eyes, with milk and wet crumbs in the thin stubble of his beard. He held a piece of corn bread soaking in a bowl of Pet Milk, the tips of his fingers in the milk covering the bread, as if hiding it from whoever was coming in the screen door.

Across the table Boyd Caswell's head raised with closed eyes that opened halfway, bleary, before his chin dropped to his chest again, as if he were staring down the front of his overalls. A quart jar of moonshine, almost empty, was on the table in front of him.

Dual's eyes shifted to Dr. Taulbee. "You recognize Boyd now you see him?"

"I sure do," Dr. Taulbee answered. "Though I'd forgot what a beauty he is."

"Boyd's resting after a hard night," Dual said. "This here is his daddy." Dual stared at the old man for a moment. "Daddy, you're losing all your pone in your milk. You ought to have Boyd fetch you a spoon."

The twelve men Dual had sent for were in the front room, sitting and standing around, some of them smoking cigarettes, patient and solemn, waiting expectantly, until Dr. Taulbee stepped in flashing his friendly smile, raising a hand in greeting and saying, "Well looky at all the good old boys are here. Boys, I heard you done it last night like genuine federal Prohibition revenue agents, yes, *sir*," Dr. Taulbee knew most of them and went around shaking hands and slapping shoulders and saying god*damn*, you all are going to enjoy your trip, I guarantee, with fun and prizes for everybody. Dr. Taulbee loosened them up and told them to make themselves at home, while Frank Long unrolled his map of Broke-Leg County and thumb-tacked it to the wall.

Long stood by the map, waiting for everybody to settle down and look his way. He recognized half the men in the room; he had pictures of them in his binder. They were stick-up and strong-arm men and ex-convicts, now in the bootleg whiskey business. Every man here was armed; two of them had brought Thompson machine guns. Frank Long was not afraid of any of them individually. But the dozen of them and Dual Meaders and Dr. Taulbee, all staring at him now, made him aware of himself standing in front of them, not part of them but with them, and he wanted to get this over with and get out as quick as he could.

He pointed out Marlett and traced the highway line east into the hills, to the spur roads that led to the areas he had circled and marked with a capital letter to indicate Worthman, Stamper, Blackwell, and Martin. He drew a line through the *W* and then pointed to the *S* for Stamper. That was the next place they'd hit, tomorrow night, unless Son Martin contacted him before then. Next, if Son didn't move, they'd hit the Blackwell place. That should do it, Long told them. By then there'd be enough pressure on Son he'd have to give up his whiskey.

They stared at the map, for a while, until one of them said, "It seems to me a long way round the mountain. Introduce me to this Son Martin, I'll make him tell anything you want to know."

Dual Meaders said, "Jesus, yes. You shoot in the knee, he'll tell."

Another man said, "What you do, you take his pants down and hold a razor over his business. I mean to tell you, you can learn anything you want."

Everybody thought that was pretty good. Dr. Taulbee made a face, an expression of awful pain and seemed to be saying, "Whooooo."

"They's some good ways," the first man said. "I like to slip on this leather glove and punch 'em around a little first, have some fun."

Frank Long waited while they laughed and talked among themselves, offering sure-fire ways of getting a man to talk. Finally, when there was a lull, he said, "We're going to hit his neighbors. We get to the man through his neighbors. That's the way I want it and that's the way it's going to be. You're playing you're federal agents and for a while these hillbillies are going to believe it; but once you start torturing people or killing without any reason, that old man sheriff or the newspaper or *some*body is going to get on the phone to Frankfort and that'll be all for the fun and prizes."

Dr. Taulbee was grinning as he rolled a cigar in the corner of his mouth, wetting it before he bit off the tip. "Frank," he said across the room, "don't worry about it, all right? They just having a little sport with you, boy, that's all."

"I want it understood what we're doing."

"We're with you, boy, don't worry."

"They're supposed to act like federal U.S. officers."

"They will."

"If Frankfort hears and wants to know who they are, I say they're deputies hired by the sheriff."

"That's good thinking, Frank."

"But they make this a shoot-up with them goddamn Thompsons, we're done."

"I believe it, Frank," Dr. Taulbee said. "that's why we're doing it your way."

"No shooting unless the stiller shoots at us first."

"Right."

"No shooting at the stiller's house, where you're liable to hit one of his family."

"No, sir, we don't want any of that." Dr. Taulbee waited, then lighted his cigar and went up to Frank Long and took him by the arm, saying, "Come on, Frank, I'll walk you out to your car."

In the kitchen Boyd Caswell was still sleeping, snoring now, but the old man was gone. Outside they saw him walking toward the privy, his withered face raised to the sun.

"It's a terrible thing to be old and poor," Dr. Taulbee said thoughtfully, blowing out a thin stream of cigar smoke. "But Frank"—turning to Long now—"we ain't ever going to become a pathetic creature like that, are we?"

"I don't aim to."

"No, sir, not if we can get that load and sell it at five dollars a fifth. What'd we say that was? A hundred and twenty-two thousand five hundred dollars. A third for you and a third for me and a third for labor and bottles. Forty thousand dollars each. Which is no bad start on keeping out of the poorhouse, is it?"

"If we can pull it."

"If we can pull it?" Dr. Taulbee seemed amazed. "What's this pulling we got to do? Frank, all we need is to trust each other and lead a clean life and we shall get our reward."

Dr. Taulbee let his grin form and gave Long a shove. "Now go on, get out of here, and see if Son's been looking for you."

Dual Meaders came out to stand next to Dr. Taulbee as Long turned around and drove out of the yard.

His gaze following the car, Dr. Taulbee said, "We're going to have trouble with that boy."

"How come?" asked Dual.

"He's starting to eat his own insides."

"He is?"

"He's getting nervous. He's starting to make rules. We don't need any of that."

"I don't see we need any of *him*," Dual said.

Dr. Taulbee seemed pleasantly surprised as he looked at Dual. "God*darn*," he said. "Isn't that something, both of us thinking the very same thing."

eight

Arley Stamper's place was raided the evening of June 18, 1931. Arley said later it was right at dusk. He saw the cars coming up his road and the first thing he did, he got his children and his old woman down on the floor and cocked his Winchester. The cars didn't show any headlights, they came sneaking in black against the trees. But how could they have sneaked past his oldest boy who'd been down by the gravel road to watch and was to give the signal? The signal being three shots. Three shots and you'd know there was hell in the air. But there were the cars driving into the yard. The men got out and they had his oldest boy with them, walking him to the house on his tiptoes with his arm bent behind his back. They had seen him and drew down on him before he could give the signal. There was nothing to do then but drop the Winchester and put your hands in the air, Arley Stamper said.

Yes, he had recognized Frank Long. The others he had never seen around here before and swore he had never sold any of them moonshine. He'd of recognized their clothes. One of them was dressed in overalls, but his hat was pulled down over his eyes and he wore a neckerchief over his nose and mouth like a bank robber. This one led them off to where the still used to be, off where the yard path went into the thicket.

Where it used to be, Arley said, because he'd moved the still. When they came back they acted sore and Frank Long asked him where the still was now. Arley Stamper said, what still? Then one of them, a big man, the one holding his boy and wearing one leather glove on his right hand, turned his boy around and hit him as hard as he could in the face. Frank Long said, don't you know what still I'm talking about? The one you moved. Arley Stamper said, oh, that still; and took them to it. They stood

142

back and one boy used a tommy gun to shoot the outfit apart so it could never be repaired. It was something to hear that gun go off, but it was an awful sight what it did to the still and the mash barrels.

No, they didn't arrest Arley—like they hadn't arrested any of the Worthmans, which was a strange thing. No, Arley said, they went on up the holler and he figured they were going to his brother Lee Roy's place.

Mr. Baylor found Lee Roy Stamper at the doctor's house in Marlett, Lee Roy clenching his teeth while the doctor closed the gash in his right arm with seventeen catgut stitches. Lee Roy said he'd put his arm through a window trying to get the son of a bitch open. But outside the doctor's house, Lee Roy admitted that wasn't the way it happened at all.

He had heard the gunfire down at Arley's and knew they would be up to his place next; so he and his wife Mary Lou's brother, R. D. Bowers, grabbed a shotgun and a high-powered rifle and got over to the still which he'd located in a gully section they had dug out and covered over with brush and vines. These federal boys had to come across a pasture field to reach them, Lee Roy said, so he and R. D. Bowers figured they would let go with warning shots to let these fellows know if they fooled around with Lee Roy Stamper they'd get their moldboards cleaned. Well, they let go, firing three shots over their heads and, God Almighty, it was like opening the door on a furnace, the fire that came back at them—bullets sniping through the brush leaves and clanging into the copper still, blowing up the mash barrels and the flake stand. When they dove for cover, Lee Roy said, he landed in a mess of broken glass and was laying there bleeding when the federal boys appeared on the edge of the gully pointing their guns at them. One of them said, well, according to the rules we can shoot these two, they fired on us. But another one, who sounded like he was in charge, told him to get a car over here and start loading moonshine. No, Lee Roy wasn't sure if it was Frank Long. No, he hadn't seen anybody with a neckerchief over his face that looked like a bank robber. Hell, the whole bunch of them looked like bank robbers. His brother-in-law, R.D. Bowers, got scratched up some and found a big wood sliver in his hip that was so deep it was like it had been shot into him. R.D. didn't say a word; he went home and nobody had talked to him since.

That Friday, June 19, Lowell Holbrook spent the morning looking for Mr. Baylor. He wasn't at his office in the courthouse; nobody was except the girl on the switchboard. He wasn't at his house. He wasn't anywhere having coffee. When Lowell went back to the courthouse, just before noon, E.J. Royce was on the telephone. Lowell waited, trying to decide whether or not he should tell Mr. Royce what he'd learned about the friend of Frank Long's staying at the hotel, this Dr. Taulbee. E.J. Royce hung up and reached for his hat. Lowell asked him if Mr. Baylor was around. No, he was out on official business. Lowell asked him if he had a minute to listen to something that might be important, or at least seemed awful strange, this man who was supposed to be a doctor but been to the state penitentiary. E.J. Royce said he would have to tell him some other time. There had been a bad accident out on the highway.

God no, it was no accident, Bob Cronin said. It's no accident when they shoot off your back tires and you go in the ditch and almost kill yourself.

When E.J. Royce got to the scene, there were cars parked along the shoulder of the road and people looking at the platform Feed & Seed truck that was tilted over and wedged against the inside bank of the drainage ditch.

Bob Cronin, age seventeen, employed by Marlett Feed & Seed, had gone out about eleven with a load of deliveries to make east of town. He was carrying rolls of bob wire, he said, and hundred-pound bags of clover seed—what was left of them. God, look at the mess to clean up.

Driving along he had seen this car up ahead parked to the left side, pointing toward town. Passing the car he had slowed up to see if it was anybody he knew, but it was three men he had never seen before, in suits. One of them was out behind the car like he was taking a leak. As Bob Cronin drove by, this one shouted something at him. Bob said he thought the man was yelling hi or making some funny remark; so Bob had waved his arm out the window and kept going. Well, actually he had given the fellow a sign out the window with his middle finger, but not meaning anything really insulting by it. The next thing he knew the car was coming up fast behind him and a fellow was leaning out the window firing a pistol at him. Bob had thought, oh my God, they must be highway patrolmen, and right away put on the brakes and started to shift down his gears. They came right up behind him, still firing and the next thing he knew he was in the ditch. When he got out, he was so scared he didn't say a word. The three of them were out of the car and one was holding a Thompson machine gun. Not him, but a littler one with a tan suit said, where are you taking that corn meal? To whose still? Bob Cronin told them it wasn't corn, it was clover seed. The one in the tan suit didn't say anything for a minute. Bob Cronin said he just looked at him, not blinking or moving a muscle in his face. A horsefly buzzed past his face and circled him and buzzed around his hair, but he still didn't move. Then he took the machine gun from the other one and fired it from ten feet away into the hundred-pound sacks, ripping them to shreds and blowing seed all over the truck and the highway. The he picked up a handful of it and said, yeah, it's clover seed all right. That was all he said, yeah, it's clover seed. They got in the car and U-turned and headed for Marlett. Bob Cronin said he heard the highway patrol had tough boys, but God, he didn't know they were that tough. One thing though, they hadn't given him a ticket.

Saturday, June 20, was the longest day of Mr. Baylor's seventy-three-year-old life. It was Cow Day and it seemed like half the people in the county were in town to buy a raffle ticket, then walk around figuring how to stretch four bits or a dollar bill along five blocks of store windows.

He hoped no boys were caught swiping candy or combs over at Kress's. He hoped Boyd Caswell stayed home and didn't weave down the street looking to pick a fight. He almost wished he might start coughing and spitting and have to go home for his wife to rub his chest with Mentholatum and stay in bed a few days. Mr. Baylor had on his desk the unofficial eyewitness accounts as told by Mr. Henry Worthman, Arley Stamper, Lee Roy Stamper, his brother-in-law R. D. Bowers, and young Bob Cronin, and he'd be a son of a bitch if he knew what he was going to do about them. Only Bob Cronin seemed within the law. (Marlett Feed & Seed wanted to know who these officers were, so they could claim damages, taking it to Frankfort if they had to.) The rest of them were moonshiners and, by law, deserved to be raided and prosecuted. He had warned them, told them to cease operating. If they didn't, then it was their funeral. That was the trouble, it was going to be somebody's funeral before it was through.

There wasn't any mention of the raids in the *Marlett Tribune*. Because it was a weekly and they'd gone to press yesterday. But next week the accounts would be on the front page and Mr. Baylor's phone would ring all day Saturday and they'd be lined up out in the hall: newspaper people from other towns; friends wanting to know was anybody hurt; friends wanting to know where they were supposed to buy it now; temperance ladies saying it was about time somebody did something.

You've got a week before the dam breaks, Mr. Baylor told himself. Rest your mind.

Two o'clock that afternoon the editor-publisher of the *Marlett Tribune* came over for the facts. Mr. Baylor let him read the as-told-by eyewitness accounts.

At two-thirty a man from the Corbin newspaper called the office.

At ten to three the manager of the Kress store called; he had this boy in his office caught stealing a black leather wrist band and a dollar-ninety-five key case, a good one.

At three-twenty a man named McClendon, who bought a farm east of town just a year ago; came in dirty and worn-out, his face bruised and swollen, to tell how Prohibition agents had burned his barn to the ground.

148

It had happened early in the morning before sunup. He hadn't heard the cars drive up, hadn't seen them till these men broke his door down and dragged him outside and started asking him where his still was.

Mr. Baylor knew McClendon had never operated a still, though he had been on a couple of Saturday night moonshine parties, including the one two weeks ago at Son Martin's place. So he asked McClendon if he had recognized Frank Long. No; and he hadn't noticed a man with a neckerchief over his face either. They kept asking him where the still was; then one of them, with a glove on, started hitting him. They asked him if he had any moonshine. He told them part of a half-gallon jar out in the barn, but that was all. They laughed when he said that, and one of them said, that's where Caz said he's supposed to keep it, in the barn.

They looked all through the barn and when they didn't find more than the half jar, this little fellow lit a cigarette and threw the match in the hay. When they were sure it was caught good, they took McClendon outside to watch his barn burn down, his wife and children watching from the house. While they were standing there, the little fellow said, next time we come, Mr. Blackwell, we want to see your still. The man said to them, Blackwell? My name isn't Blackwell, it's McClendon. The Blackwells live three miles from here. The little fellow shook his head and said, no wonder he didn't have any shine in his barn.

Mr. Baylor was pretty tired by now. He told the man to keep quiet about what happened; because if they wanted to, they could send him to Atlanta on the strength of his having that half jar. It's a shame, Mr. Baylor told him, but Jesus don't go writing to your congressman about it, get busy on a new barn.

When McClendon had gone Mr. Baylor took his glasses off and rubbed his eyes, seeing little white spots floating around in the dark. He'd pull the shade and try to take a nap for ten or fifteen minutes.

At quarter to five the phone woke him up. Lowell Holbrook, calling from the hotel, said Bud Blackwell had shot and killed a man out in the street not five minutes ago.

Bud Blackwell and Virgil Worthman came to town that Saturday afternoon with loaded .38s and twenty-four jars of moonshine. They parked the pickup truck back of Marlett Feed & Seed where the farmers would drive in to load their supplies. By four o'clock Bud and Virgil had sold out their stock and drunk a quart of the stuff between them.

Virgil had gone to get something to eat, but Bud was still back of the store when Mr. McClendon came out and started loading building supplies into his truck. Bud asked him if he was going into the contracting business. Mr. McClendon told him no, but he would be willing to build the Blackwells a new barn for a good price. Bud said they didn't need a new barn and Mr. McClendon said not to be too sure if he had not been home all day. After Mr. McClendon told him about the men coming and thinking it was the Blackwell place, Bud began to curse and swear that if he saw any of them he would teach them to fool around with a Blackwell. Well, Mr. McClendon said, he thought he saw one of them over in front of the hotel as he came by. Mr. McClendon followed Bud through the feed store out to the street. They walked down to a cafe where Bud went in and got Virgil Worthman; then they walked on toward the hotel where, from across the street, Mr. McClendon pointed out the car parked in front and the man sitting behind the wheel. The man was one of them who'd burned down his barn, Mr. McClendon said.

Lowell Holbrook told Mr. Baylor about the shooting, as he had seen the whole thing from the front door of the hotel.

About a half hour before, two men had come into the lobby: the one who was about to be shot and another one, whom Lowell had seen before, a short guy in a suit that was too big for him. The short guy went up the stairs to the second floor, probably to see Frank Long. The other one waited in the lobby for about fifteen minutes, then went outside and got in the car. He was sitting there when Bud Blackwell and Virgil Worthman came across the street and walked up to the car.

Lowell didn't hear what was said. Bud

Blackwell was close to the car door, between this car and the one angle-parked next to it. Virgil stood back-aways, almost in the street, his hands in his pockets. Bud Blackwell seemed to be doing the talking. When he turned from the door Virgil Worthman walked on across the street. Bud was following him, but when he got into the middle of the street— there was no traffic at that moment—he turned to the car again and yelled something. The car door came open and the man started to get out, reaching into his coat with his right hand. That was when Bud Blackwell shot him, as the man was half out of the car. Bud fired three or four times and then ran across the street. Lowell didn't see where he went. The next moment there were cars in the street and people out on the sidewalk wanting to know what had happened and some of them pointing toward the car. The short guy came out of the hotel right past Lowell Holbrook. He stuck his head in the car, leaning over the man who'd been shot, then pushed him over and got in behind the wheel and drove away.

Mr. Baylor went into the hotel to call the doctor. The doctor said no one had been brought in with a gunshot wound, but he would let Mr. Baylor know if they did. Mr. Baylor told Lowell Holbrook not to talk about the incident until he had made an official statement. Then Mr. Baylor went home; he sat down in his easy chair with the crocheted doilies on the arms and drank four ounces of

Son Martin whiskey while his wife fixed him a nice supper.

He didn't want to have to go out to the Blackwells.

He didn't want to have to talk to Frank Long.

He wanted to go to bed.

His wife told him he looked like he was coming down with something. If he didn't rest it would knock him flat and he wouldn't be any good to anybody. So Mr. Baylor didn't go out to Blackwell's or look for Frank Long. It was too late this evening and tomorrow was a Day of Rest. He'd do it Monday.

Sunday afternoon, June 21, a delegation of neighbors and moonshiners came out to talk to Son Martin.

They all arrived at the same time, two old cars and two pickup trucks nosing cautiously up out of the hollow and rolling into the yard, careful of the foxhounds dodging in front of the wheels. The men got out of the cars—wearing their Sunday overalls and coats and shirts buttoned at the neck—and assembled in a straggling group, looking toward the house but holding back. None of them seemed in a hurry to walk up to the porch or get a step ahead of the others.

Son counted fourteen men; no women or children present, men and grown boys: Worthmans and Stampers and their kin, Mr. McClendon and some other people Son didn't know very well. Virgil Worthman was next to his dad. No Blackwells though—thank God for small favors. Son moved to the kitchen table and replaced his pistol in the drawer. Aaron had leaned the 12-gauge against the wall by the stove. He said, "You have more company in a week your daddy had in ten years."

When Son walked out on the porch they nodded to him and Mr. Worthman explained they had stopped by on their way home from church service.

"Now just the men go?" Son asked him.

No, they'd had a meeting after the service and these here fellows had agreed to come out and speak with him.

Son waited.

"We understand you're still making whiskey," Mr. Worthman said.

"Some."

"Then they haven't closed you down."

"Not yet."

"Well, they've closed the rest of us down; all but the Blackwells and we understand they're next."

"I'm sorry to hear it."

Virgil Worthman said, "You don't look sorry to me. You look like a man that don't care what happens to his neighbors."

Son didn't pay any attention to Virgil. He said to Mr. Worthman, "If there's something I can do, to get you started again, I'll be glad to help."

"There's only one thing you can do for us," Mr. Worthman said, "You know what that is."

"Give them my whiskey."

"The hundred and fifty barrels. It's the only way they'll leave us alone."

"It's that easy, uh?"

"I'm not saying it's easy. I'm saying how it is. If we build new stills they'll bust them again."

"Then hide the stills."

"Now you're making it sound easy," Mr. Worthman said. "Like if they don't find anything they'll go away. These federal people mean business. The aren't going till they get what they want."

"You think they're federal people?"

"They say they are."

"I say I was, would that make me one?"

Virgil Worthman was squinting up at him. "Who do you say they are, they're not federal?"

"Bootleggers," Son answered. "Gangsters hired to do a job on us."

"Your friend too?"

"I don't know about Frank Long, if he's real or not."

"Say it's true," Mr. Worthman said. "What do you do about it, call the law for help?"

"All right, if you were standing over here," Son asked, "what would you do? If you banked your future whiskey —knowing you could sell it for enough to buy good land or a business somewhere—what would you do?"

Mr. McClendon spoke up. "I'd look to see what it was doing to my neighbors," he said, "to people aren't even making moonshine but are suffering because of it."

"Everybody is certainly ready with advice,"

Son said. "Come on, Mr. Worthman, what would you do?"

"I'd give them the whiskey, Son."

"Mr. Stamper, what would you do?"

"I've seen them," Arley Stamper said. "I tend to agree with you thinking they're bootleggers."

"You'd give it to them."

"Yes, I would."

"Well, I'm not going to," Son told them. "They can try and take it, but I'm not *giving* it. You can come to me like it's all my fault, I'm still not going to give it to them. You want my advice—if I was standing where you are—I'd decide if I wanted to run a whiskey still or not run it and then I'd do one or the other. But, Jesus, I wouldn't go crying to anybody about it."

They stared up at him solemnly. Arley Stamper turned and walked through the group and the others began to follow him, walking over to the cars and pickup trucks.

"Son," Mr. Worthman said, "you don't have a family. That's the difference."

Son went into the house. He stood at the screen door until the cars were out of the yard and he could hear the hounds chasing them down the road.

"You didn't have to talk to them that way," Aaron said.

The yard was still, dust hanging in the sunlight. "What would you do?" Son asked

"I don't know," Aaron answered. "But I wouldn't have talked to them that way. They your friends."

Son turned away from the door. "We'll see," was all he said.

The doctor called Mr. Baylor early Sunday morning: a man with a gunshot wound had been brought to him late last night. The bullet had entered his side beneath his left arm, smashed a rib and tore a hole in his back coming out. If the man went to bed and didn't move, he would probably be all right. But the one who'd brought him in said, wrap him up good, Doc, because he's going to Louisville tonight. The doctor said the man couldn't be moved, but this little fellow insisted his friend wanted to go to Louisville to see his own doctor. Mr. Baylor asked him if he had the man's name and address. The doctor said yes, but he believed it wasn't his right name. No, neither of them said they were federal agents.

The editor-publisher of the *Marlett Tribune* called up later to find out what was this about a shooting in front of the hotel? Who had been shot? Was it true Bud Blackwell had done it? Mr. Baylor said he had not finished questioning people and for the editor-publisher to hold his horses and call tomorrow or the next day.

You can't hide or run away, Mr. Baylor told his wife, and started to put his pants on. But his wife pushed him back in the bed and said she would have his son and grandsons come over and tie him to the bed if she had to. Mr. Baylor said well, he wouldn't mind seeing

157

his grandsons—weren't those boys the captains though?

Monday morning Mr. Baylor slept till seven-thirty, then got dressed and ate a good breakfast. He'd had all day yesterday and last night to decide what he was going to do. The first thing would be to see Frank Long and ask him some questions about these federal agents he had working for him. What district were they from? Where were they staying? How come they didn't arrest anybody? What happened to the man who'd been shot? If Frank Long's answers sounded fishy, then by God he'd call Frankfort and find out what the hell was going on.

Before Mr. Baylor left the house E.J. Royce called him. They'd just got word the Blackwell place had been raided during the night. Mr. Baylor swore and told E.J. to pick him up. They'd better get out there.

nine

Monday morning Dr. Taulbee and Dual Meaders were out in the Caswell barn looking over the whiskey that had been taken in the raids: mostly quart and half-gallon fruit jars and a few gallon jugs of moonshine with Coca-Cola labels.

"Not too bad for the work put in," Dr. Taulbee said. "What'd you get last night?"

158

"Just the few cases there," Dual answered. "They came shooting, we had to get out of there."

Dr. Taulbee frowned. "They drove you off?"

"Like they was waiting for us. We got to the still and commenced to smash it, and they let go from the bushes."

"Wasn't anybody hit?"

"Well, one boy was. I don't think too bad."

"What about the one Saturday?"

"Somebody's driving him to Louisville and is coming back with more men, like we talked about."

"Is he going to make it, the one was shot?"

"I don't know. But we'll have these others anyway."

"Maybe you should go back to this Blackwell place tonight. Finish the job."

"I was thinking that," Dual said. "Or start on Son Martin and quit wasting our time."

"You think you can bust him?"

"We go over there again I'll take care of him. Both of them."

"Both of who?"

"Him and his nigger."

"Do you think the nigger knows where the stuff's at?"

"That's what I'm going to find out next trip over there."

"It does seem like we're wasting some time," Dr. Taulbee said. He turned as the door opened and sunlight came into the enclosure. Frank Long stood in the doorway.

Dr. Taulbee said, "Hey, Frank, how you doing, boy?"

"We got something to talk about," Long said.

"Well, fine." Dr. Taulbee moved toward him. "Speak up, don't be bashful."

"I want to talk to you alone."

"We're alone. It's only Dual here with us."

"He's what I want to talk about mainly."

"Then he should hear it, shouldn't he?"

"I'll say it to his face if you want," Long said. "He's messing up this deal, him and his gunmen."

"Frank, you said you wanted guns."

"I said it had to be done my way or the whole thing will come down on us. All right, they shot up a feed truck. They burned down a man's barn, wasn't even a stiller. They have a gun fight on the main street on Saturday afternoon—"

"You don't care for this business," Dual said, "what're you in it for?"

"Frank, when boys are carrying guns there's the chance they're going to go off," Dr. Taulbee said, like explaining it to a small child. "We know there's the chance somebody might get hurt, right?"

"And that somebody might get caught," Long said, "and start talking."

"Frank, we got that boy out of here was shot Saturday. He's home in bed."

"And the one last night," Long said. "Is he home in bed?"

"There's something I haven't heard about? Which one is that?"

"Boyd Caswell," Long said. "Have you seen him around here this morning?"

"Dual"—Dr. Taulbee turned to him—"what's he talking about?"

"You asked me was anybody hit, I said yes."

"What's he talking about!"

"Boyd Caswell got shot last night."

"Where is he now?"

"I'm not sure exactly—"

"You left him there? Jesus, of all the people you leave Caswell?"

"I didn't know at the time." Dual was frowning; he'd never heard Dr. Taulbee speak loud to him before. "We got out of there once we seen they had position on us. I guess it wasn't till we was back we noticed Boyd wasn't along."

"You left him!"

"We didn't *leave* him. It was just he didn't come back with us."

Dr. Taulbee stared at Dual. Then he put his hands in his pants pockets and walked deeper into the dimness of the barn. He turned around and came back and said, with only a slight tight edge in his tone now, "Dual, you're going to have to go out and get that boy."

"He might be dead, all we know."

"Yes, he might be," Dr. Taulbee said. "Or, he might be sitting up in bed telling them we're not federal agents at all, but just some old boys from Louisville."

"Well, what could they do about that?"

"They could tell the sheriff. They could do that, couldn't they?"

161

"I guess."

"Then the sheriff, he could pick up the telephone and call the state capitol, couldn't he do that?"

Dual nodded slowly, thinking about it. "I guess he could. Listen, I better get a couple of cars and go back out there."

Dr. Taulbee was his old self again, swatting Dual on the shoulder as he started past him. "Hey, Dual, now you're talking. Go get him, boy."

The old man, Mr. Caswell, was standing in the yard facing the barn. As they came out, his head raised to them, following their sound.

"Boyd?"

Dr. Taulbee and Dual walked past Mr. Caswell; they didn't seem to notice him.

"Boyd, is that you?"

Frank Long hung back. He hesitated, then took the old man by the arm and walked him toward the house.

"I haven't seen Boyd all morning," the old man said. "The lazy som-bitch is supposed to give me my breakfast."

"Come on, we'll get you something. Nice dish of pone and milk."

"Lazy som-bitch, he's dead drunk, ain't he?"

"He's all right," Long said. "They're gone to fetch him."

"See, we knew they were coming," Mr. Black-well explained, "because of what they done over at McClendon's Friday night."

Mr. Baylor and E.J. Royce followed Mr. Blackwell out to the still, located in a limestone cave, and back to the yard while he described how they had beat off the revenuers. You bet they were ready for them. Right after supper the women and small children had been sent over to Raymond's place to be out of the way. They cleared the house, set Bud out by the road as a lookout, while the rest of them—Mr. Blackwell's three younger sons, his three brothers, and an uncle who'd come over to help out—hid in the rocks by the cave. Along came Bud soon after dark to say the revenuers were turning up the road. Well, they waited and fired everything they had and chased them through the pines and back to their cars, then fired at the cars until they were out of sight down the road. Probably some of them had been shot; though there was only one they had been sure of hitting, because they had him and he was bleeding all over the ground back of the house.

Boyd Casswell was lying in the shade of a beech tree, a neckerchief loose around his neck and the front of his shirt and overalls stained with blood. He was the one who'd been leading them to the stills, Boyd Caswell, who'd probably drunk more of their whiskey than any man in the country. Well, he wasn't going to be drinking any more.

Mr. Baylor said to E.J. Royce, "Bring the car up here." When Mr. Blackwell asked him what he planned to do, Mr. Baylor said,

"Take the man to the doctor, what in hell you think I'm going to do?"

Bud Blackwell said, "Hey, now wait a second. We pumped five rounds in the son of a bitch to kill him, now let him die."

"And you pumped a round into another man Saturday," Mr. Baylor said, glaring at Bud Blackwell, "which you are coming to my office to tell me about. But right now just get the hell out of my way."

They got Boyd Caswell into the car, across the back seat, though he didn't open his eyes and Mr. Baylor didn't hold much hope for him. He glared at Bud again and told Mr. Blackwell to see that his son came in or he would swear out a warrant for his arrest on a charge of murder. With E.J. Royce at the wheel they drove away, taking it slow out of the yard so as not to jounce Boyd Caswell and start him bleeding all over the car.

As soon as Dual Meaders saw the car approaching them, still way down the road, he knew it was coming from the Blackwell place. This lonely stretch, a pair of ruts winding through the backwoods, didn't lead anywhere else; so the car had to be coming from there. If they were Blackwells they'd even up the score for last night. If it wasn't Blackwells they'd look and see who it was.

This was a good spot to take them, with trees and scrub falling away to one side and a steep bank on the other. Two cars could pass here,

164

but barely. Though no cars were going to be passing right now. Dual braked, easing over to the right shoulder, then swung the wheel sharp to the left and came to a stop angle-parked across the road as the oncoming car started blowing its horn, the driver leaning on it and not letting up. Dual had three men with him. They didn't ask what was going on. They kept their eyes on the car ahead of them and got out. One of them went back to the car behind, that was carrying four men, and now they all came up on both sides of the road, a couple of them moving around behind the blocked car.

When the horn stopped blowing there wasn't a sound until, further down the road, crickets started up in the dusty weeds along the ditch.

"Take a look," Dual said. He stood in front of the car, two faces staring at him through the windshield.

The man who approached on the driver's side paused with his hand on the door and motioned to Dual. "In the back," he said.

Dual walked over and looked in at Boyd Caswell. He studied a moment, making sure he was still breathing, then shook his head and began to smile. Walking back to the front of the car he was still smiling; he couldn't help it and didn't care who saw his teeth.

But now the old man with the glasses was getting out the passenger side, holding the door open in front of him and pointing to the gold-lettered inscription, tapping his finger hard on the door sill.

"You see these words?" Mr. Baylor said. "If you can't read, it says Sheriff's Department, Broke-Leg County."

"I can read," Dual said. "You better get back inside, papa."

"You better show me your identification, then get your cars the hell out of our way. We got a prisoner needs a doctor's attention."

"He ain't going to make it," Dual said.

"You going to get out of my way?"

"I'll tell you what. You can give him to us and we'll take care of him."

"And you can throw your tail up in the air and hump at it," Mr. Baylor said, "because if I don't take this man in nobody does."

"You're right that time, papa," Dual said. He drew his revolver and shot Mr. Baylor three times through the chest, then emptied his gun at the windshield, at the face staring at him with eyes stretched wide open and the mouth trying to say something. "Somebody else will have to finish off Boyd," Dual said. "I'm empty."

They pushed the sheriff's car off the road and watched it roll down the slope, plowing through the brush clumps and snapping off the young trees.

ten

Tuesday, June 23, Son drove into town to buy meal and stores.

He went to the grocery first, where he always bought his sugar, and asked for three hundred and fifty pounds. The clerk went out into the back room and returned and said they didn't have any sugar. Through the doorway Son could see the fifty-pound bags stacked up. He said, I can see the sugar, right there.

The clerk said yes, it was sugar, but it had been special ordered by somebody and couldn't be sold to anybody else. Son asked to speak to Mr. Hanks, the owner of the store. The clerk, trying to act natural, looking Son straight in the eye, said Mr. Hanks wasn't in today.

At Marlett Feed & Seed Son ordered eight bushels of yellow corn meal, a hundred pounds of wheat bran and a fifty-pound can of lard. The manager asked if he wanted to pick it up in back. Son looked at him and said didn't he always pick it up in back? The manager said he'd tally it up then. Son told him to put the amount on his account. The manager was polite but he didn't seem to have an expression of any kind on his face. He told Son he already owed a hundred and eighty-seven dollars and he would have to pay it before he charged any more items.

"How long have I been coming in here?" Son asked him.

"I don't know. A few years I guess."

"My family's been coming in fifteen years. All of a sudden our credit isn't any good."

"It's a new policy," the manager said.

"Since when?"

"We got to pay our bills too, you know."

"Since when is this new policy?"

"Just recently; the past week or so."

"Since the day before yesterday," Son said. "All right, I expect you know what you're doing, because you're never going to see me in this store again."

"It's a new policy," the manager insisted.

Son went to the bank and had to wait twenty minutes for the manager to get back from his dinner, then had to wait some more while the manager sat at his desk behind the fence and looked through papers. The open room was quiet; Son was the only customer in the place. He listened to the overhead fans for a while and every few minutes heard the bank manager clear his throat.

Finally Son got up and stepped over the fence. He said, "I want to borrow three hundred dollars. You going to give it to me or not?"

The bank manager looked up at him. He didn't say hello or, well, Son Martin, how're you doing? He said, "What have you got for security?"

"A producing still," Son answered.

"You know we can't accept that."

"How about forty-five hundred gallons of whiskey?"

"There's no such thing as whiskey these days," the bank manager said.

"How about my place?"

"I don't know what it's worth."

"Do you want to have somebody look at it?"

"Well, we're pretty busy right now."

Son could hear a fly close to him in the silence and the whirring of the overhead fans. He stepped over the fence and walked out.

At the Hotel Cumberland he again had to wait. The girl came out of the office to tell him Mrs. Lyons was tied up at the moment, but would be with him as soon as she could. He picked a chair away from the sunlight coming in the window and lit a cigarette. Then watched Lowell Holbrook coming down the stairs. Lowell didn't look over right away. He stood by the desk. Then when he did look over, Son was staring at him and saw his reaction; the sudden look of surprise and Lowell's eyes shifting away, but coming back now because he knew he had been caught and would have to acknowledge Son's nod. But he didn't come over until Son motioned to him.

"How're you doing, Lowell?"

"Pretty good, I guess."

"I'm waiting on Mrs. Lyons."

"Yes, sir, I figured you were."

"She's busy doing something, I don't know what."

"Yes, sir. Well, I better get back to work."

"Lowell, I wondered if I could have a glass of cold water."

"You can get one in the dining room,"

Lowell said. He crossed the lobby to the desk. Behind it, he leaned over the counter with a pencil in his hand, like he was checking a list of something. His head would come up and he would look out toward the front door, concentrating, deep in thought.

When Kay Lyons came out of the office, Lowell nodded toward Son and pointed the end of his pencil in that direction. Son watched her crossing the lobby, raising her eyebrows and putting on a little expression of surprise.

"What brings you to town?" She stood in front of him.

Son looked up at her. "Everybody's busy today. Did you know that?"

"It was something I had to finish."

"No, I mean everybody. Everybody's very busy. And serious. Boy they're busy, serious, hard-working people in town. I never realized before how busy everybody was."

"Is that what you wanted to tell me?"

"No, I wanted to ask you something."

"What?"

"If you'd loan me three hundred dollars." He kept his eyes on her. He watched her eyes move away and come back and saw the little raised-eyebrow look of surprise again.

"Why would you want three hundred dollars?"

"I need it."

"That's a lot."

"You told me you've got over four thousand dollars in the bank."

"Well, yes, but that's my husband's insurance money. I mean he left it to me and it's all I have."

"When we get married, is it still his insurance money?"

"That's different—listen, tell me why you need it."

"To buy stores."

"Well, don't you buy on credit?"

"Not any more. I found out today my credit's run out."

Her eyebrows closed together in a frown, then raised again. "They won't give you credit? I don't understand."

"Yes you do."

He waited, watching her, but she said nothing.

"I have to be a good boy," he said then, "and do what people want or else they start talking it over and saying, 'What kind of a neighbor is this man? He isn't any neighbor, he's only for himself and doesn't care about others.' Then they say, 'Well, a man like that sure doesn't deserve to run a credit. He won't be nice to the people he lives among, we won't be nice to him.' "

"Well?" Kay said.

"Why don't you sit down."

"I have to get back to the desk."

"Will you loan me three hundred dollars?"

"I told you—it's insurance money. I have to be very careful."

"Kay, yes or no?"

"All right. No."

"Don't you think I'd pay you back?"

171

Kay had stopped dodging, trying to, evade him. "How would you pay me back?" she said. "Lying in a grave next to your father, how would you pay me? Would you leave it to me in your will? Three hundred dollars worth of bootleg whiskey, is that how you'd pay?"

"It's to have things out in the open," Son said, "isn't it?"

Kay sat down now, on the edge of the sofa facing his chair; her hands were locked together on her lap, but her face was relaxed now and her eyes did not wander from his.

"You know what I want," Kay said. "I want to leave here. I'll leave tomorrow if you want to go and I'll give you every cent I have in the bank. But I'm not going to give you money to help you stay here and kill yourself. Wouldn't I be foolish to do that, pay for something I don't want?"

"Kay, you're not buying me. We leave here together it's got to be when I can take what I want with us. What *I* want. Doesn't that mean anything to you?"

"What you want isn't possible."

"I've got to find that out for sure. I'm not giving it away to anybody, not to federal people and least of all not to anybody pretending to be federals."

"What do you mean by that?"

"I don't think the ones making the raids are agents, I think they're bootleggers."

"Are you sure?"

"No, it's what I think."

172

"If it's true, it could be worse, couldn't it?—what they might do."

"I don't know. It's up to them."

"But either way, no matter who they are, you can't win. Because what you want isn't possible."

"That's the way your uncle and the rest of my neighbors see it," Son said, "so I guess I can't explain it to you either. But I'm staying. They'll put me under or get tired and go away, I'm staying. You want to wait around and see what happens, it's up to you."

Miley Mitchell didn't like going out to that farmhouse. She didn't like looking at the old blind man. He was depressing; the whole place was depressing and filthy dirty. The men would sit around looking at her, not being able to do anything about it. Once one of them said to her, "You ought to be upstairs and we could take our turns." And she had said, "Gee, that would be a lot of fun," and walked away from him. She could picture the old stained mattress crawling with bedbugs. No thank you. Dr. Taulbee said, then stay at the hotel if you don't like the place. They had been here nine days now and nine days were about eight too many in a town this size. Once you had walked five blocks up the street and five back and had dinner in the hotel dining room, you had been to Marlett. Sitting in the lobby had been kind of fun the first time; aware of the salesmen looking her over; though not one had worked up enough nerve to walk over and start a conversation. Even a dry-goods salesman could help pass the time. The fun would be in getting away with it without Dr. Taulbee knowing; the salesman letting her know he was a pretty slick article and not realizing he could get shot if they were caught. She had gone to the beauty parlor Friday for a wash and wave set. Saturday, Sunday, Monday, Tuesday—four days ago. She might as well go again today; get out of the hotel room before she started counting the designs on the wallpaper.

It was either while she was going down the stairs or walking across the lobby that Miley decided against the wave set. She just didn't think about it again once she saw Son Martin and the hotel woman talking. He was saying something and she was listening, at least not interrupting, not smiling either. Neither of them looked this way. The hotel woman never did smile or touch him; she got up and walked away.

Miley didn't wait for Son to notice her, she went out to the sidewalk and stood at the curb with her back to the hotel entrance. When he came out she followed him to his pickup truck; she opened the door and got in as he sat with his hands on the wheel staring at her, but she didn't look at him until she had closed the door and sat back with her hands in her lap.

Now she gave him a nice little smile that showed in her eyes and waited for him to say whatever he was going to say.

But he didn't. He didn't say a word. He looked at her for a moment, then backed into the street and drove west out of Marlett, past the stores and the church and the filling stations, past the section of old homes and trees lining the street, and out into the open sunlight of corn fields and telephone poles and shadowed hills in the distance.

Miley wasn't sure what she wanted to happen. She did feel it was working out better than she would have predicted. She had pictured Son getting mad and telling her to get out or asking her if Dr. Taulbee was sending a girl now to do his work—being grim and solemn about it—or saying something dumb, sarcastic, like this isn't a taxi, lady, or where is it I'm supposed to take you? Nope, none of that. He drove along at forty miles an hour, looking straight ahead, not saying one word and Miley felt a little excitement and settled down to see what would happen, deciding once they were out on the highway, she wasn't going to say a word either and they'd see who could hold out the longest.

What happened, after about ten minutes Son turned off the highway and came to a stop in a dense glade of trees. He helped Miley out of the pickup, helped her take off her clothes, spread his shirt on the ground for her to lie on and eased down next to her. At one point Miley said, "Oh God—" and a little while later, when he was stepping into his pants and she was looking up at him, not ready to move quite yet, she said, "I guess you win."

Son was yanking the end of his belt through the buckle. "You bet," he said.

"What're you mad about?"

"I'm not mad."

"You can tell that by your big smile."

"I'm going to Corbin. You want to come?"

"When are you coming back?"

"I don't know, tonight if I can get what I want in Corbin."

"God, I don't know why you couldn't."

"You want to come or not?"

"I'd have to think of a good story to tell him."

"Like he doesn't know you're with me."

Miley made a face, a hint of disappointment. "Don't say anything dumb, okay? Up to now you've been perfect. I'll tell you truthfully he doesn't know where I am and he didn't put me up to this."

"Then what'd you come for?"

"I don't know. I guess just to see what you're like. Say, do you go with that woman at the hotel?"

Son hesitated. "You could say that. Why?"

"She's not your type." Miley waited, but he didn't say anything. "She's too nice for you."

"What does that mean?"

"Did you ever bring her here? She'd die. She has to have everything nice. You can tell by looking at her."

"I better take you back."

"If you want me to go to Corbin with you, I will."

"What will you tell him?"

"I don't know. I'll say I went for a walk and got lost in the woods."

"Are you—married to him?"

Miley smiled. "You're sweet."

"You like him?"

"He's not my type but he could be worse."

"Well, what're you living with him for then?"

"I guess I haven't had any better offers." Miley got up slowly and handed Son his shirt. "Would you care to make one?"

"Like I don't have enough trouble."

"Maybe I could help you. I don't know."

"Put your clothes on."

"Nervous?"

"Somebody's liable to come along."

"You didn't worry about that before. Come on, are you the strong silent type or aren't you?"

"How could you help me?"

"Well"—Miley stepped into her skirt— "let's see. I know enough about that big teddy bear to send him to jail for life. How's that?"

"He's a bootlegger, isn't he?"

"You haven't made an offer yet," Miley said.

"He's no more with the government than I am. Neither is that little mule shooter."

"Dual. Isn't he a cutie?"

"The one I'm not sure about is Frank Long."

"Well," Miley said, "make an offer and if it's any good I'll tell you about the doctor and Dual and Frank and the whole bunch." She turned her back to Son. "Zip me."

"You've told me," he said, "Just admitting there's something to tell."

She came around, standing close, her face raised to his. "Then why don't you call the police? You can't, but I could, couldn't I?"

Son touched her face, holding it in his hand. She was a good-looking girl with soft skin and nice mouth and warm green eyes. And if you let her talk any more, Son told himself, you'll begin to believe her.

He dropped her off in front of the Baptist Church, turned around, and headed for Corbin as fast as the pickup would go.

eleven

Tuesday evening, a little before seven, Frank Long was in his hotel room waiting for Dr. Taulbee to call or come by or do something. He had been waiting all day for Taulbee to "think over the situation." Because the window was open a few inches to get some air in the room, Long heard the people below in the street. He didn't hear actual words, only the urgent sounds of words and the sound of hurried steps on the sidewalk. Long went to the window, pressed his forehead against the glass, trying to look straight down, then raised the window and looked out, leaning over the sill.

People were bunched around a pickup truck parked at the curb. In the box, lying side by side, were three bodies. Long recognized Boyd

Caswell and the sheriff, Mr. Baylor, who seemed to be looking straight up at the window. A hat covered the face of the third one.

Long closed the window. He walked down the hall to 210 and knocked on the door. Miley opened it after he waited and knocked again.

"Is he here?"

Miley stood with her hand on the door. "I haven't seen him all afternoon."

"Where would he be, at the farm?"

"I guess so, I was out." Miley turned away from the door, pushing it open. "Unzip me, will you?"

Long hesitated a moment before following her into the room. Then he was close behind her, pulling down the zipper of her blouse, looking at her bare white skin. Miley said over her shoulder, "You can wait for him if you want. I'm going to take a bath."

"I might do that," Long said. "You think he'll be coming soon."

"He could come any minute." She turned, looking up at him. "Or he might not be here for an hour. I never know what he's going to do."

"Well, it's pretty important I see him."

"There's a bottle of liquor on the shelf in the closet."

"You want some?"

"I don't drink," Miley answered. Going into the bathroom and closing the door part way, she began to undress behind it. Long could hear the water running. He kept looking at the door, catching brief glimpses of her body, knowing she was expecting him to come in. He went over to the window: the people were still gathered around the pickup truck. What the hell were they waiting for? Why would they have the bodies on display in front of the hotel? Like they were waiting for him to come out and show him and say, "See what you done?"

Somebody would have to investigate it. Maybe the town police or the county prosecutor or whatever law enforcement they had here. They would sit down and start asking questions.

Miley was singing something he had never heard before—a soft, little-girl voice—making sounds for the words she didn't know. She's going to ask you to hand her something, Long told himself. He'd go in and there she would be looking up at him, her big white boobies floating in the water. All wet and soapy waiting for him to reach in and grab her.

Like hell, he said to himself, and went back to his room.

Inside of ten minutes his suitcase was packed and he was at the desk in the lobby to check out.

Mrs. Lyons looked a little surprised and he almost told her he'd received a call from his office and had to leave right away; but he caught himself in time, knowing she could check on his calls, and didn't tell her anything. She was saying she was sorry, but he would have to pay for tonight also, even though he wouldn't be here—when Lowell Holbrook came over.

"They took them away," Lowell said.

Frank Long turned to him, easing against the counter. "I could see something from my window—what was going on?"

"They found the sheriff and E.J. Royce and Boyd Caswell all shot dead."

"You don't tell me."

"Yes, sir. They said it looked like Mr. Baylor and E.J. were bringing Boyd in and he got one of their guns and they shot it out, killing each other. They came here looking for the undertaker. He was having his supper."

"That's why they were out in front?"

"Yes, sir, looking for the undertaker," Lowell said. His gaze dropped to the suitcase. "Excuse me, but are you leaving?"

"Yeah, have to leave."

"They say it might have been moonshiners done it, besides Boyd Caswell."

"I'll have your total in a minute," Mrs. Lyons said. She walked off toward the office. Long watched her: she didn't seem too concerned and it surprised him. Three men were dead she must have known, but she went about her business and didn't even seem interested.

"Do you believe it could have been moonshiners?"

Frank Long's eyes came back to Lowell. "I guess it could."

"I don't know any of them would have shot Mr. Baylor."

"Well, maybe it was Boyd Caswell, like you said."

"Maybe."

"You got police here to look into it?"

"Just a constable," Lowell answered. "Mr. Baylor was the law. With him dead I don't know who it would be. I wondered maybe if you were going to do something about it."

"No, that wouldn't be my department. You know what I am, huh?"

"Everybody knows it."

"I expect people are talking about us raiding the stills."

"Yes, sir," Lowell said. "Since you're going, I guess you must be through raiding."

"I'm through," Long said.

Lowell watched him pay his bill, then touch his hat to Mrs. Lyons and walk out. Lowell didn't offer to help him with the suitcase. He watched him go through the door before he turned to Mrs. Lyons.

"Did he say where he was going? Back to Frankfort?"

"I didn't ask."

"It seems funny. Three men are killed and he leaves the same day. Don't you think that's kind of funny?"

"I don't think about it at all," Mrs. Lyons said.

"I mean you can't help but wonder."

"Yes you *can* help it," she said then, with a note of irritation that took Lowell by surprise. "You can keep your nose out of it and let them all kill each other. That's what you can do." Mrs. Lyons turned from the desk and went back to her office.

"Long's coming," Dual said.

Dr. Taulbee got up from a chair and followed Dual through the kitchen. Out on the porch they watched Frank Long walking over from his car. Dr. Taulbee got his grin ready.

"Hey, Frank, I was fixing to come see you."

Long reached the porch. "Has he told you about killing the sheriff?"

"Dual? Sure he did."

"It doesn't seem to bother you any."

"Well, what was he going to do? That old man had Boyd Caswell in the back seat. He ever held a bottle in front of Boyd and started asking questions, it would be all over before breakfast."

"It's all over now," Long said.

"What're you talking about? Listen, Frank, Dual didn't have any choice. He seen what he had to do and did it."

"That old man pulled his gun me," Dual said. "I shot him too dead to skin."

"And then you finished Boyd."

"I didn't want to, he was a buddy of mine. But he was going to die and there wasn't anything we could do to help him."

"That's what I mean," Dr. Taulbee said. "He didn't want to shoot Boyd or that old man but, Frank, if he hadn't, you'd be heading for Atlanta next month. Heck, Dual saved your hide and you haven't even thanked him for it."

"I don't dare look at him," Long said, 'I'm

liable to grab him and wring his neck. We had a good plan that could have worked, but he starts shooting people and now we might as well piss on the fire and call the dogs."

Dr. Taulbee nodded, "I guess your part in it's done. I don't see any reason for you to stay around."

"I mean it's over for all of us."

"No, sir, Frank, it's over for you, but we got to find us that whiskey yet."

"If he pulls his gun," Long said, "I'll shoot you first."

"Nobody's talking about shooting any-body." Dr. Taulbee sounded hurt. "I'm saying it's time for you to go home is all."

"I guess it was going to come sometime," Long said. "I should've known the day you got here."

"Well," Dr. Taulbee said, "You can't know everything. You took a chance and you didn't make it. Dual here doesn't trust you. He's for putting you under; but I told him, old Frank's not going to sic the law on us. He knows if we get put in jail he's going to be right there with us, hoping and praying some accident don't befall him. Isn't that right? I said to Dual hell, Frank was nice enough to tell us about that boy's whiskey, what do we want to hurt him for?"

"I guess that's it then," Long said. "Since there's not much I can do about it."

"There isn't anything you can do," Dr. Taulbee said, "outside of wish me luck. This next raid I'm leading myself."

Dusk was settling as Long drove away from the farmhouse. Reaching the gravel road he flicked on his headlights.

He told himself that he must be awful dumb. Taulbee must think he was about the dumbest boy he'd ever met. He had called Taulbee in and now he couldn't do a thing about it. What he couldn't figure out was why he had trusted Taulbee in the first place. Probably because he figured he had a hold on Taulbee and, if the man pulled anything, he'd put on his federal agent hat and arrest the son of a bitch. He hadn't thought about Taulbee having a hold on him at the same time. Maybe he should have stayed in the Army. Son Martin had said something about that, about staying in the Amy where there was somebody to think for him. That hadn't made him mad at the time, but it did now, thinking about it, because he could picture Taulbee laughing at him and saying the same thing. Boy, he would sure like to think of a way of nailing Taulbee and that loony-head Dual and the rest them. He had stayed calm and walked away, because he looked stupid enough without crying and kicking his feet and, because if he'd stayed any longer, he would have taken a swing at Dual and gotten shot full of holes before he cleared the yard.

Passing Kay Lyons's house he thought about her for a moment, picturing her, the dead expression on her face as he checked out—probably a cold fish underneath her woman's body; no life in there at all. The house, he noticed, was completely dark.

But there was a light farther down the road, off to the right side. He couldn't figure where the light was coming from: the church was down there and the cemetery.

It was a lantern hanging from the stubby limb of a tree. As he drew near the cemetery he could see the dull light beyond the fence and a man digging a grave. It was strange, like he had seen a lantern in a cemetery before somewhere, a little while ago, though he knew it had not been around here. Then he remembered what it was: the grave of Son Martin's father with the light post over it, a lonely grave up on the hill, all by itself.

Long stopped, skidding in the gravel, then backed up until he was even with the lantern light and saw the grave digger looking over toward him. The man leaned on his shovel as Long got out and came through the fence.

"See you're working late."

"They's going to be some burials tomorrow."

"That's what I hear. I knew one of them."

"Boyd Caswell? I see you're coming from that direction."

"That's right. You knew him?"

"I knew them all that's buried here. Them or their children or grandchildren."

"I used to know that girl was married to Son Martin," Long said.

"She's over yan side of that big gravestone

there. Her and Son Martin's old mother lying side by side. Next to them's his daddy's folks and I believe two little brothers passed on as babies."

"The whole family," Long said. "Except his dad."

"It's the family plot," the gravedigger said.

Long got in his car and drove on, asking himself, If they are all buried there, then why is that old man all by himself up on the hill? Answer me that.

Lowell got a pot of coffee and some cookies from the dining room and took them in to Mrs. Lyons, who was in the office making entries in a ledger book. She was not in a talkative mood and hadn't been for a few days, so Lowell didn't waste time trying to make conversation.

He went out to the lobby just as Frank Long was coming in the door with his heavy suitcase.

"Did you forget something?"

"No, I'm checking in."

"You just left here a half hour ago."

"Well, I got to thinking, since I've paid the room for the night I ought to get my money's worth, oughtn't I?"

"You'll have to check in again."

"I don't mind."

"How long you 'spect to be?"

"Oh, I don't know," Frank Long answered. "Probably just a short visit this time."

twelve

Son didn't get home from Corbin until almost noon Wednesday. He had spent the evening with his father-in-law, Mr. Hartley, and finally stayed at his house that night. In the morning he asked Mr. Hartley if he would loan him three hundred dollars. The man wrote out a check without comment or question. Son thanked him and left. He bought his sugar and grain in Corbin and, on the way home, stopped off at Marlett Feed & Seed to pay his past-due bill, counting off one hundred and eighty-seven dollars in front of the store manager, not saying one word, and walked out.

It was a dry, sunny day that June 24. The open yard and the outbuildings lay still in the noon heat. Son came to a stop by the porch. He turned off the ignition and sat there a moment in the stillness. In broad daylight it was quieter than night. There was no breeze and nothing seemed to move. What Son wanted to know right away: where were the hounds? How come they hadn't chased him up the road? Maybe it was always this still at noon on a hot day and he hadn't noticed it before. But he still wanted to know where those hounds were. Aaron was probably up at the still. The hounds could be with him; though Son couldn't remember Aaron ever taking them up there.

He went into the house. There was a pail of water on the sinkboard and a pot of coffee, that smelled fresh, on the stove. He was upstairs, taking off his suit coat and about to change into work clothes, when he heard the hounds faintly, way off. By the time he got downstairs and out in the yard, Aaron was coming across the pasture. The were close in front of him and Aaron's arm was extended, like he was pointing at them. It looked strange until Son realized Aaron had them on a rope leash. It was something else he couldn't remember Aaron ever doing. Or going hunting at noon; though Aaron was sure as hell carrying the 12-gauge.

"You get anything?" Son asked him. He reached for the hounds as they panted and sniffed and jumped up on his legs.

"We got us plenty," Aaron said.

Son looked at him, straightening, "Who'd you see?"

"They up in the woods."

"Who is?"

"The ones your friend brought. I saw one of their cars. I heard other ones making noise in the woods, 'Hey, where you at? Man, I'm *lost*!' They don't know what they doing up there, but I know what they come for."

"Why didn't they drive in the road?"

"I don't know that. I think they know you was away and they want you to come home and think everything fine before they come get you. But I took these two boys and sniffed like I was squirrel hunting and it ain't any surprise now."

"Maybe we still have time to get out of here."

189

"Is that what you want to do?"

"They've probably closed the back door by now."

"Sealed off the road. Nobody in or out," Aaron said. "Then they sneak up."

"Or they watch for a while. Think maybe we want to take some whiskey and make a run."

"Where'd we run to?"

"I don't know of anywhere," Son answered. "So I guess we stay."

Aaron nodded, at ease. "We here when they come."

They got ready for Dr. Taulbee, knowing he was watching them: two small figures through field glasses three to four hundred yards away: two boys doing the chores, taking their time in the afternoon heat.

They unloaded the pickup truck, carrying what looked like grain sacks into the house. And inside they stacked the heavy sacks beneath the two windows facing the open yard.

They hauled a load of old lumber from the barn to the porch. Son Martin looked like he was repairing the porch steps, replacing some of the boards. Yes he was, through from three to four hundred yards you would never see he was wedging in the two middle steps and not nailing them. And you would never see Aaron, who was pulling lumber inside from off the porch and covering the two offside windows that faced the near slope behind the house.

Throughout the afternoon, every hour or so, they would carry a pail of water into the house until they had half-filled a thirty-gallon barrel.

On the kitchen table, pushed over closer to the windows, they laid out their weapons: the 12-gauge Remington and two rifles, a lever-action Winchester and an 0-3 Springfield, and all the ammunition they had in the house. Son put his Smith & Wesson .38 in his back pocket.

They parked the pickup truck on the offside of the pump in the yard, to give them some protection if they had to go out there again.

They pulled back the linoleum in the kitchen and pried up a couple of floor boards so Aaron could drop down into the cellar and bolt the door that opened from the outside. Then he pickaxed the hard-packed floor and shoveled the dirt into grain sacks and handed them up to Son.

At suppertime they ate biscuits and gravy and green beans and wondered if there was anything else they should do. If they had some bob wire, Aaron said, that'd be good, string it around the place when it got dark. They'd bring the dogs in the house. They'd stay by the windows and keep watch on the yard, because maybe those boys out there were tired from waiting and would feel like doing something. They'd be a moon tonight, Aaron said; that was good.

They went out to the porch after supper, to sit down and smoke and watch the hill slopes fading in the dusk, spreading their shadows over the pasture. The ridges were silent and almost black against the night sky. Son finished another cigarette and flicked the stub out into the darkness.

"What do you think?" he said.

"I think they decide to go home or come visit us," Aaron said. "They no reason to stay out in the dark."

A little while later, inside the house, in the kitchen, Aaron rose from where he was seated by a window.

"All the getting ready we done, I forget the mule."

"The mule's all right," Son told him.

"It don't have any water I know of. If it be awhile before we bring any out there, that old mule be thirsty."

Son looked out the window, at the moonlight that lay in the yard between the house and the deeply shadowed outline of the barn.

"Take the water out of the barrel," he said, "you won't make any noise at the pump." Within a few moments he was watching Aaron crossing the yard, his shadow following him until he was close to the barn and enveloped in silent darkness. Son heard the door creak and saw a faint movement. Aaron was inside.

Son waited. He knew how long it would take to walk through the barn to the stock pen and pour a bucket of water into the trough. As the minutes passed he told himself Aaron had decided to stay there awhile and keep watch from the barn. They could sneak up from that direction, using the barn for cover. Or they could have already done it and were inside the barn when Aaron walked in. After about ten minutes more, Son had to know for sure. He opened the door about a foot, letting the foxhounds run through the opening and down the steps. He watched them sniff around the yard. As they worked closer to the barn, they would sniff, then raise their heads and stand still. The hounds were about ten feet from the deep shadows, when they started growling, then barking and howling, raising a racket to frighten off whatever the unknown thing was inside.

Son didn't see the half door in the barn open or make out the figure there until the repeating shotgun went off four times, louder than the howls that came from the dogs as they were cut down by the charges. By the time Son got his Winchester on the door it was closed and the deep shadow lay in silence.

Dual held out the shotgun. "Here, take it."

"I can't see where you're at."

"Then light the goddamn lantern. He knows we're here now, it don't matter."

"I guess you got them, I don't hear anything."

"Course I got them—what'd you think I was going to do?"

Aaron said, "They wasn't hurting you any."

"Jesus," Dual said, "who asked you anything?"

A gloved hand held a lighted match inside the lantern until the wick caught and the yellow glow showed Dual holding the shotgun and the heavy-set man with the glove and Aaron standing with a rope that was noosed tightly around his neck, reached up over a

193

horse-stall beam and hung slack behind him falling to a tangled coil on the floor.

The man who took the shotgun from Dual reloaded the magazine, then trained the barrel on Aaron.

The heavy-set man, with the glove on his right hand, went into the stall behind Aaron. He took a good grip on the slack end of the rope, coiling it around his hands. "Ask him again," he said.

Dual moved in close to Aaron. "You going to tell us?"

"I can't tell you if I don't know, can I?" Aaron gasped and reached up as the rope tightened, pulling him up off the floor. The heavy-set man strained, leaning away from the rope, turning to get it over his shoulder and raise Aaron's feet another few inches from the floor.

"You should tie his hands behind him," the man with the shotgun said. "He's trying to pull himself up."

"Trying," Dual said. "You try raising yourself. In a minute your arms start waving crazy. Okay, Carl."

The heavy-set man turned, letting go of the rope and Aaron dropped to his knees.

"Hey, nig," Dual said, "you going to tell us or not?"

"I work for him; I don't know about no whiskey."

"We hear you helped make it."

"No, sir."

"Pull him up again."

"What if he doesn't know?" the one with the shotgun said.

194

"He knows."

"But what if he doesn't? Then he can't tell us. But the one inside the house can."

"Jesus Christ," Dual said.

"Listen, I mean we tell the one inside. He gives us the stuff or we string up his boy."

"Yeah?" Dual said, "then what?"

"Then he gives us the stuff."

"He gives us the stuff?" Dual was frowning, because maybe he didn't understand it right. "Why would he give us the stuff? All he's got to do is get himself another nigger."

The linoleum came up easier this time when Son rolled it back; the floor boards were already loose; all he had to do was lift them out. He took the Winchester and the 12-gauge Remington with him, dropped them to the floor of the cellar and lowered himself down through the hole. With the weapons he went up the steps to the slanting outside door, opened it as quietly as he could, and stepped outside. To his left was the corner of the house. Beyond it, several yards, was the pump, and beyond the pump the dark shape of his pickup truck, sitting in the open about thirty yards from the barn. Son stayed close to the house, listening. When he was ready he cradled the weapons in his arms and crawled on his elbows and knees out to the pickup.

"Take him up to the loft," Dual said. "There's a beam sticks out over the door; loop the rope around it and hold him there and we'll be right up."

The heavy-set one went up the ladder first. He said, "Come on," and Aaron followed, the rope trailing from his neck.

Dual said to the one with the shotgun, "We'll ask again. If he don't tell us, we run him out the door."

"Hang him," the one with the shotgun said.

Dual shook his head. "That ain't any fun. See we don't tie the end of the rope. But he don't know it. We run him out and get a wing shot at him while he's in the air. Buddy, like shooting crow."

"What if you miss him?"

"Miss him? Listen, you stay down here. When I give you the word, I'll say *now*. You pour it into the house and keep Son off us."

"Then if you miss the nig I can bust him, huh?"

"Miss him?" Dual said again. "Buddy, you got something to see."

Dual climbed the ladder, up into the darkness above the lantern. A crack of moonlight showed the edge of the loft door, not closed tightly. Dual positioned Aaron about ten feet from the door, facing it. He moved back to where the heavy-set one had tied the end of the rope to a support post, whispered to the man to untie it and hold it loose in his hands, ready to let go when he gave the word.

"Your last chance," Dual said to Aaron. "Or you go through the door with rope around your neck. You'll fall aways and then *snap*, the rope jerks tight and breaks your neck. You want that, it's yours."

196

"No, sir," Aaron said, "but I can't tell something I don't know."

"Well, it's up to you." Dual glanced back at the man holding the rope. "You don't want to tell us, then get ready to run, nig."

Dual drew his .38. He got a step behind Aaron, waited a moment, and yelled, "Now!" pushing Aaron, running him toward the closed loft door. The timing was dead on, the automatic shotgun opened up on the house as Dual stopped short and Aaron banged through the door, his arms reaching for moonlight. Dual fired twice and instinctively ducked back as the solid reports of a rifle filled the yard below.

Aaron had his hands in front of him as he hit the door and was through it falling and grabbing frantically for the rope above as the gunfire erupted like it was all around him, like he was falling into it, and he hit the ground so hard the jolt went through his body, buckling his legs and throwing him forward. He got up to run and fell and started crawling and heard somebody say, "Aaron!" as the shotgun skidded across the ground and the stock bounced and hit him in the face. He knew the voice and knew the shotgun and knew what to do with it, grabbing it and finding the triggers as he rolled to his back and saw the figure in the loft door and let go one 12-gauge charge and the second on top of it and saw the figure pitch forward and hit the ground like

197

a sack of meal. Aaron could make out the pickup; he was crawling toward it, hearing the rifle going off close to him, then Son had him by the arm, raising and running him around behind the pickup to the cellar entrance. He fell down the steps and lay breathing in the darkness with an awful pain shooting up his legs through his knees, but he still had hold of the shotgun. Son almost had to pry it out of his hands.

During the night Dr. Taulbee left Son Martin's still and moved in closer, to a position in the rocks and brush above old man Martin's grave.

All the goddamn shooting and then silence. Nobody had come back from the barn, so he didn't know what happened outside of a lot of guns going off. Maybe Dual had him pinned down and was moving in for the kill, the little fellow squirming up close to the house and inside before they knew he was there. Maybe. Dr. Taulbee wanted to know what the hell was going on; so he sent five men down with two Thompson machine guns and moved to a closer position to see what he could see. He watched them go down the hill, circling to get behind the barn. In a couple of minutes they were down among the dark shapes and shadows and Dr. Taulbee had to wait again. Though not long this time.

The gunfire came as suddenly as it had before, the Thompsons going off now, tearing apart the stillness, sweet music that was good to hear and set a grin on Dr. Taulbee's face as he stared expectantly into the darkness. There were rifle shots and again a Thompson rattling the night. Then silence.

The first of the five to return had trouble locating Dr. Taulbee in the rocks. Dr. Taulbee had to call to him. The man came stumbling up the gravel slope out of breath.

Taulbee couldn't wait any longer. "You get them?"

No, the man didn't think so. There wasn't any way of telling.

"Then what the hell was all the shooting about?" Well, the big guy, Carl, was in the barn and the boy with him was shot dead. They didn't see Dual right away. They said to Carl come on, show us where them two are. Carl pointed out the pickup truck and both the boys with Thom let go at it until their magazines were empty. That should do it, one of them said. The five spread out in a line and went over to the pickup truck that was shot through like a sieve. When they looked in and didn't see anybody, my God, it was a terrible feeling being out in the open and knowing the two were in the house. It was either go back to the barn or rush the house—there wasn't room for all of them behind the pickup truck. Since nobody had fired at them so far, they decided to rush the house. The two boys with the tommy guns commenced to shoot at the windows, one of them going ahead, running right toward the porch up the steps. But he never got up. It was like the steps collapsed under him and as he fell these two rifles opened up from both windows and everybody dove for the pickup truck. The boy by the porch was so close under them he was able to crawl out; all they had done was shot his hat off and grazed his skull. Nobody else was hit; they laid down cover fire with a Thompson and got back to the barn.

There, the others were coming now: the big guy, Carl, and the other four carrying two people and having a struggle getting up the slope. Dr. Taulbee called out, "You find Dual?"

Nobody answered until they were up in the rocks. Then one of them said, "We got him here," laying him down in front of Dr. Taulbee, "but I don't think he's moved."

Or ever would. Dr. Taulbee could tell by Dual's eyes he was dead: the fixed, wide-open stare, like somebody had given him the surprise of his life. It made Dr. Taulbee tired to look at him . He gazed down at the dark shape of the house for a while and then at the men waiting for him to say something. Then made them wait a little longer.

"Well," he said finally, "what I want to know, are you all going to bring that boy out of there or do I have to get somebody else to do it?"

The big guy, Carl, said, "Tomorrow, we're going to bring the nigger out dead and the other one with his hands in the air."

"I want to see that," Dr. Taulbee said. "Because to now it doesn't look to me like you've scared him one bit."

thirteen

Upstairs, in the bedroom directly over the kitchen, Son used a big auger to drill through the floor plank and the board and batten ceiling below it. With his eye close to the hole, he could look down into the kitchen and see one of Aaron's swollen ankles extended out from where he lay against the grain sacks.

It was Thursday morning, June 25. As soon as Taulbee's men opened up on the house with rifles, snapping the shots in from the dense tree cover of the slope, Son went upstairs with a pair of field glasses. Crouched low, his glasses on the window sill, he studied the ridges and rock strains, making out movement here and there, but not seeing anything worth aiming three hundred yards to try and hit. They had better keep their bullets for the close-in business that would come as soon as Taulbee realized the snap shooting wasn't doing any good, not telling him anything. The bedroom, his own, was a good place to watch from. Son drilled the hole so he could call to Aaron in a hurry if they came across the pasture. Aaron had stayed awake most of the night and was trying to sleep now, with his knees turning blue and his feet and ankles swollen up like he had eight pairs of socks on.

Son kept his gaze on the slope because he wanted to see the first sign of a move from them.

Taulbee was probably in the stillhouse, giving orders. And Frank Long, where would he be? He hadn't been in the barn last night, though he might have been with the bunch that came later. They'd got one of them; Son had heard the man yell, as he went through the steps. The sight to see again was Aaron blowing Dual out of the loft with the 12-gauge. That was one of them would never have to be shot again. Son was sure of it, though at first light they saw he wasn't lying in the yard.

A bullet went through the window, shattering the glass above him. Son continued to study the slope through the field glasses. It was hard to tell where the shots came from. The snap shooters were spread out in the trees. He would hear the far-away reports and the bullets hitting fragments of window glass and thudding into the timbered walls. They were telling him he wasn't getting out of here unless he gave up. Well, as far as Son was concerned, the first part could be true. He might not get out. But there was no chance giving up. He was sure of that.

Until he saw the cars appear on the ridge.

Inching his glasses across the hills and gulleys, he stopped on an open, grassy part of the slope. A car was parked there in the sun. It was a good hundred yards to the left of where Taulbee's men were hidden in the trees. Still, Son decided, it was probably one of their cars. Maybe a few more shooters had been called in.

Two more cars appeared. Son watched the men get out and he almost jumped up and yelled to Aaron because they weren't Taulbee people at all, they were boys in overalls and farm hats and goddamn if they weren't looking this way and figuring it out and deciding what to do. Son swung his glasses back to the trees and said to Taulbee, "Look over there, mister, and see what you're going to have on your hands."

As another car and a pickup truck drove across the open slope, Son got down by the hole in the floor and called, "Hey, Aaron, look out over to that open piece, see who's coming!"

Son put his glasses on the ridge again. God Almighty, there were a dozen men up there now.

And a couple of women.

He couldn't understand why the women would be here. Less they wanted to see Taulbee run so bad they couldn't be kept home.

Now there was a wagon coming off the ridge trail, holding up a car behind it, and a stake truck from Marlett Feed & Seed that looked like it was loaded with men.

Son kept his glasses on the stake track. He watched men jump off the back end and saw young boys climbing the sides to get down. He counted several more women and young girls in the group. He inched his glasses over the slope and noticed a few other women he had missed. He saw the men standing in groups talking. He saw a couple of others spreading a blanket on the ground. He saw a man handing some folding chairs down from the stake truck. He saw friends, neighbors, acquaintances, and people he didn't know sitting and standing around on the open ridge in the June sun and he didn't see a rifle or a shotgun among the bunch of them.

They had come out to watch.

They had lost their stills because he had not given up his whiskey. Now they had come to see it taken from him.

Son turned from the window. He sat on the floor with his back to the wall, in this room where he was born and where he had slept almost every night for the past four years. He felt tired and his head ached. He hadn't slept more than an hour. He hadn't eaten since yesterday supper, though he wasn't hungry. He sat in the bedroom with his back against the wall and began wondering what in hell he was doing here, getting shot at, putting on a show for his neighbors.

That's the fact of it, Son thought. Whether they are up there watching or not anywhere in sight, what you're doing is putting on a show. Showing off. It's your whiskey and nobody can take it. So they tell how you never gave up and somebody says well, where is he now? And they say, he's buried, where do you think? Buried? You mean they killed him? Of course they killed him. Then he was awful dumb not to give up, wasn't he?

Well, he was brave.

Well, some call it brave, some call it stupid.

The only thing Son was sure of, he was tired. Sitting in the upstairs room looking at the bed—he'd like to get in it and pull the covers up over his head and stay there. But he had to decide something, what was brave and what was stupid. How he wanted people to talk about him. Or whether he cared or not.

Bud Blackwell and his dad and Virgil Worthman and a few other men were in one group. They squatted and sat in the grass at the slope of the ridge, where the hill fell away in a sweep of weeds and brush toward the pasture. They squinted in the noon glare and gazed around at the other groups, and occasionally one of them would get fidgety and rise up to stretch and spit tobacco. It seemed like it would be something to watch but, Jesus, there wasn't much happening.

The other groups felt about the same. One boy said if they didn't start something soon he was going home and pick bugs off his tobacco. Some others were getting hungry. They should have packed lunches, they said. A couple of the men had moonshine jars they were passing around, but nobody, it looked like, had thought to bring water. Somebody said, well, there's Son's pump right down there, and the ones near him got a kick out of the remark. Bob Cronin, from Marlett Feed & Seed, said he had a tarp in the truck; maybe they could rig up a tent as a couple of old ladies—fanning themselves with pieces of cardboard—looked like they were about to pass out. Finally they sent a boy over to the Worthman place to bring some water back.

A man would look out over the pasture toward the Martin place and give his opinion of the situation. Son was treed and there wasn't anything he could do about it.

Virgil Worthman said, he couldn't get out by the road down the holler, they'd laid trees across it to box him in.

Bud Blackwell said, down the holler? Shit fire, look at his truck. He couldn't drive it over to the privy.

What the federals ought to do was get up on the slope back of the house, light a hay bale, and drop it on the roof. Burn out.

Drop it on corrugated tin, yes, sir, that was a swell idea cause everybody knew how tin burned.

It didn't look like any tin roof.

If it didn't then somebody needed glasses. No, the only way was to rush him or starve him out.

How long did anybody figure that would take? Son didn't look like he ate much anyway.

They'd have to rush him and that would be the show to see.

Somebody asked who had seen the Bengal Lancers picture and they got to discussing tortures, like sticking bamboo slivers under a boy's fingernails to get him to tell where something was. Maybe they'd do it to Son if they'd seen the picture.

The closemouthed son of a bitch, you could hardly get to tell whether he thought it was going to rain or snow.

Somebody said, hey, look, and they all looked toward the house. No, over there coming out of the trees—tiny little ant figures running across the pasture, circling wide to get on a line behind the barn, four of them running in a single file, hurrying hunch-shouldered, the first one gradually gaining distance on the others. Everybody was watching the four men now. They heard the thin report of a rifle from the direction of the Martin house. They heard a muffled echoing report up in the sandstone rocks and they saw the first man go down and lay there, my God, dropped in his tracks from a good three hundred yards. They watched the other three men stop, looking toward the house, run back as fast as they could to the cover of the trees. They were hidden from sight before anybody on the ridge moved or looked around. One man whistled softly and shook his head. He had a funny, startled look on his face. Others stared out at the tiny dark shape lying in the pasture but nobody spoke for a while.

They would look over at the trees, but they didn't expect to see anybody come out of there again in the daylight.

Lowell Holbrook had got a ride out in Bob Cronin's stake truck. Lowell was the first one to notice Frank Long. He hadn't seen him come; it must have been while they were watching the four men; but there he was. His car was parked just in from where the road came out of the trees into the open and he was standing by the door looking out over the hood, studying the Martin place and letting his gaze drift over to the wooded slope, getting the lay of the land. Lowell wasn't sure what to do, whether he should go over and say anything to him or not. Finally he didn't have to do anything.

Bud Blackwell saw Long. As soon as he did, he walked over with Virgil Worthman and a group came trailing behind.

Long threw them off balance. He nodded and said, "I've been looking all over for you. I was out to your place and Worthman's before I learned everybody was out here watching." Long looked out at the pasture, then let his gaze move over the cars and groups of people in the clearing.

"Yes, I see a crowd of people watching, but I don't see nobody helping."

Bud shifted his weight, staring narrow-eyed at Frank Long. He wasn't sure what to say now, though he had part of it in mind and said, "It would look to me like you're in the wrong part of the woods. How come you're not leading your men?"

"I'll give you a simple answer. Because they're not my men any more. They quit me to do it themselves and told me to go home or get put under." Long paused. He had them, they were staring hard at him and he felt only a little tenseness inside. "You wonder what I'm talking about, all right, I'll tell you. Those people over in the trees aren't federal agents at all. See, I wanted to do this job by myself; so I hired some boys, like deputies you might say."

Bud Blackwell and the others were listening, not moving their eyes from him.

"You can understand I got a job to do, to the whiskey stills. Now then, I figured if I didn't call in any more federal people I'd get all the credit myself. That was bad thinking. But the worst part, I picked the wrong deputies and they want to shoot everybody they see. Well, I got to do a job, as I said. But not if it means shooting at honest men trying to make a living. You follow me?"

If they followed, no one was admitting it. They were letting Frank Long talk.

"I'm here to tell you," Long said, "I made a mistake of judgment. Those people after Son are cutthroat killers, every one of them, and you're standing here watching while they try to murder one of your own boys."

He wanted a short silence, to give his last words time to sink in. But Mr. Worthman spoke up. He said, "You're telling us this. A week ago you tell us you'll bust every still in the county if Son doesn't hand over his whiskey."

"Because," Frank Long said simply, "I thought it would be the way to avoid bloodshed."

"Our old uncle shed blood that very night," Mr. Worthman said.

Long nodded solemnly. "I know, and that's when I began to learn these people are killers and I'd made a mistake. A man can make a mistake."

"He surely can," Bud Blackwell said, "and you made your big one coming here thinking we'd help Son Martin. You want us to run the

bad boys off so you can get down to bustin'
stills again."

"No, sir—"

"So you can go after Son's whiskey yourself."

"No, I'm telling you the truth. If you don't
help Son right now, they'll kill him."

"And you won't ever find his whiskey."

"I'm thinking of *him*."

"Well, bein' you're so thoughtful," Bud
Blackwell said, "ought'n you be down there
with him?"

It took a couple of seconds for Virgil
Worthman to catch on; then he couldn't help
smiling. "Sure, he's a friend of Son's—how
come he ain't helping him?"

"That's what I mean," Bud said. "He comes
up here, says he sees a crowd of people
watching, nobody helping. Well, I know one
son of a bitch is going to help."

Lowell Holbrook watched them take hold of
Long, a bunch of them crowding around so that
Long was hidden for a minute. Then they had
both of Long's arms twisted behind and were
running toward the slope of the ridge. He was
holding back, but not fighting; he was trying to
say something. "Let me take my car down!" he
said. God, thinking of his car.

They pushed him down the slope and he ran
stumbling and then rolled aways, losing his hat
and getting his suit covered with dust and briars.

He stood on the slope looking up, brushing
at one sleeve. "Let me get my suitcase," he
called out. "All right?"

Virgil Worthman had gotten his shotgun from

the car and was aiming it at Long. "You'll get some thing else," he said, " 'less you start a-running." Long turned after a moment and started down the hill, brushing at his clothes.

Lowell watched him, thinking about the suitcase and the BAR rifle inside.

fourteen

Aaron's shoulder was against the grain sacks, his Winchester pointing out the kitchen window. He looked over as Son came down the steps carrying the Springfield.

"You see who's coming?"

"Frank Long."

"How come you didn't shoot him? I 'spected to see him go down about at the stock pen."

"He's coming to join our side."

"Tha's nice," Aaron said.

Son opened the door as Long reached the porch. Through the field glasses he had picked out Long on the ridge and had watched them gang him and throw him down the hill. He said, "Watch the steps."

Long strolled in looking around the room, at the shattered windows and bullet scars in the walls and cupboards. He was in no hurry. Finally, when he looked at Son, he grinned and said, "How you doing, buddy?"

Son almost smiled. "Not working out like you thought, is it?"

211

"Buddy, I couldn't stand to look at that man any more. I come to help you run him off your land."

"Those people up there"—Son nodded toward the ridge—"they wouldn't help you, uh?"

"They got funny ideas, those people."

"Dr. Taulbee, he threw you out, too, I guess."

"We parted company when I learned he was nothing more than a bootlegger."

"You mean when he told you he'd have you shot if you didn't start running."

"Something like that," Long admitted. "But as you can see I didn't run, did I? No, sir, I've stayed to help you beat him."

Son watched him. "You've stayed for more than that."

"Well, you might say I've stayed to protect my interest."

"Your interest in what?"

"That's right. I haven't told you we're going to be partners." Long kept looking at Son with his easy, almost smiling expression. "We might as well be. Since I know where the whiskey's hid."

As Aaron said, "*Now* look-it what's coming—" Son turned to the door and as he saw it—the car bouncing and swerving coming fast down the slope from the ridge—he heard Frank Long say something and then almost shout it, "That's my *car*!"

It looked like the same one, coming dead on toward the house, cutting through the pasture

212

weeds with a wispy trail of dust rising behind. They could hear the rattle of it and the sound of the engine, then the high whine of rifle reports as the car reached the yard, swerved toward the barn, and came around in a wide circle to pull in with the driver's side next to the porch. Lowell Holbrook looked up through the side window, his hands gripping the wheel like he was afraid to let go. Son got him out of there and Frank Long got the suitcase from the back seat. Once they were in the house the rifle fire stopped.

Lowell still looked scared, even as Frank Long patted him on the shoulder and said, "Boy, I think you got a tip coming."

"I don't know," Lowell said. "I don't believe it, but I guess I'm here."

Long had the suitcase on the floor now, like a boy pulling open a birthday present. "You sure are here," he said. "You and Big Sweetheart."

Son took a seat, resting his arm on the table, watching Lowell and Frank as he lit a cigarette. The boy had a good reason for coming or else he wouldn't be here. So there was no sense in asking dumb questions when it appeared the answer was in the suitcase. When he finally saw what it was—as Frank took out the parts of the BAR and began fitting them together—Son waited.

He waited until the weapon was assembled and Frank was holding it up before he said, "I've got a few things to say about this party we're having, which I don't remember inviting anybody to. I've got some other things to say

213

about this partnership you mentioned, Frank. But first, I think you better move your car out of the way, else Big Sweetheart isn't going to do you much good."

"That's sound advice," Frank Long said.

It was. Not twenty minutes later Dr. Taulbee came down on them.

"Jesus Christ," Virgil Worthman said, "look at the cars!" He jumped up as the first car came out of the trees wobbling from side to side, easing along in the ruts. The men squatting with him got up and people in other groups, seeing two cars coming toward them, moved out of the way and stood watching. There was an old lady a boy had to help; somebody else snatched her blanket from the ground before the first car reached it.

There was no doubt who they were, the cars coming out of the trees from that direction, from the trail that led around to Son Martin's still. But when Bud Blackwell saw there were just the two cars, with what looked like three men in each, he took his time moving aside and the driver honked his horn at him.

"You had enough?" Bud said. "You all going home now?" The man in the back seat of the car nosed a tommy gun out the window and Bud shut up.

As the cars crept by Virgil Worthman said, "They're going for something. Jesus, I thought for a minute they were coming at us, but they're heading out."

"Like hell," a man near Virgil said. And somebody else said, "They're going right the same way Lowell Holbrook did!"

They were, too, following his tire tracks in the weeds, straight down the slope.

Frank Long said, "Well, here we go, boys," and turned the BAR in the direction of the cars.

He had taken over Aaron's window—once he'd pushed his car away from the porch—and swiveled the BAR around in the window sill, letting the sights roam over the yard and the barn. Holding the gun on an angle out the window, he could train it on the rocks above old man Martin's grave and sweep left into the trees. Dr. Taulbee was in for a surprise.

Lowell Holbrook was on the floor. Son and Aaron were at the second window, facing off the porch with a clear view of the two cars coming at them on a line from out of the pasture. The cars didn't belong to anybody in Marlett, Son was sure of that now, and Frank Long confirmed it. "Taulbee's fastest cars," he said. "But you can bet the doctor ain't in either of them."

Son could make out the barrel of an automatic shotgun sticking out the front window of the first car. He suspected the machine gun would be in back, but didn't see it until the first car was swerving at the corner of the house to cross in front of them and he was firing the Springfield at the sunspot on the windshield and Aaron's Winchester was going off in his ear as the BAR opened up, filling the room with its hard-pounding racket. Son was aware of a Thompson fixing from the first car, but now he was swinging his front sight to the second car, firing twice to empty the clip, then brought up the Smith & Wesson to let go at the car's side windows. Now Aaron had emptied the Winchester; he grabbed the Remington and fired both barrels fast, without putting the gun to his shoulder, and the BAR kept pounding away. Son watched the first car veer off out of control and go through the front of the barn. The second car was running for open country with Long's BAR chasing it until the pan was empty and, in the silence, they watched the car bump and scrape its way to the far side of the pasture. Two men got out and ran for the trees. There were no sounds from the barn. Past the shattered frame of the opening, the rear end of the car was barely visible in the dimness.

They reloaded and sat watching the barn. Son looked over at Frank Long a few feet away, then let his gaze move outside again. He said, "Where do you think the whiskey's hid?"

Long answered without looking over. "Under your old daddy's grave."

Son could feel Aaron and Lowell Holbrook watching him. "A hundred and fifty barrels," he said. "That would be some hole."

"If you dug it straight down," Long said, looking at him now. "But if the grave is sitting on a mine entrance or an air shaft, then it's something else."

"That's what you think, uh?"

"I think it's funny the old man is buried up there by himself when the rest of your kin are down in the graveyard."

"That's where he asked to be buried."

"You say it and people believe it. Like the light over the grave, you say he wanted it because he died in the dark of a mine shaft." Long turned from the window. "I say you rigged the light so you can keep an eye on your whiskey when it's dark."

Son watched him get up from the window and look around the room, the BAR under his arm now.

"What're you looking for?"

"The switch."

"Right behind you, on the wall."

Long turned. The light switch was near the window. He stooped then. "The tommy guns tore up your wall, didn't they? You can see the wires where they come in from outside.

As Son rose he glanced at Aaron, whose eyes shifted briefly and returned to Long. Past Long's shoulder they could see where the window frame and wall planks had been splintered by gunfire. Long pulled away fragments of wood, then worked a board loose and twisted it out of the wall.

"It might have shot up your wiring," he said. His back was to them as he looked closely into the opening. "You've got a number of wires in there for one light post, haven't you? I see two wires coming in. One goes up to the switch. What's this other one for?"

"I guess it used to be part of the house wiring," Son answered. "Goes down to the Delco outfit in the cellar."

Long straightened, leaning the BAR against the wall. "It doesn't look like it to me. I learned wiring in the Engineers same as you did."

Son kept watching him. "Probably for something my dad had hooked up."

"You're telling me a story now," Long said. "That wire comes in from outside." His eyes moved over the wall. "Runs along there—I'd say over to that cupboard." He walked past the stove to the other side of the room; stooping, he opened the lower doors of the cabinet.

"Can goods," Son told him.

"That's all I see."

Long remained stooped, feeling inside. He jiggled the bottom board, then pushed the cans aside and lifted the board, wedging it against the shelf above it.

Aaron turned from the window, letting the barrel of the Winchester rest on Long. Son didn't move or take his eyes from the man.

"Well, now," Long said, "look-it here." He glanced over his shoulder, then noticed Lowell Holbrook watching and motioned with his head. "Boy, you ever see one of these?"

Lowell came over. He didn't know if something was going to jump out of that dark space or what. "Get closer," Long said, and Lowell hunkered down next to him.

"Know what it is?"

218

"It looks like some kind of a box."

"What's it look like with this handle in the top?"

Son straightened slightly. "Be careful now."

"He means it," Long said. "For if I was to push down—"

Lowell knew what it was now. "It's a dynamite thingumajig—an exploder!"

Long looked over at Son, grinning. "That's what it is all right—hey, Son?—a dynamite thingumajig, like we used to have in the Engineers. Boy," he said then, "why do you suppose he'd wire up to his old daddy's grave?"

"I don't know," Lowell said. "To blow it up?"

"You believe he'd blow up his daddy's remains?"

"No, I don't think so."

"No, sir, his daddy ain't in that grave. Is he, Son?"

Son hesitated. "You're telling it."

"All right, I'd say his daddy's buried some place else. That grave, what looks like a grave, covers up an old mine shaft that tunnels into the hill, and that's where the whiskey's at, set with charges, so that anybody was to dig there and find the whiskey, Son pushes the plunger and *boom*, nobody gets it. How many sticks you got in the hole, Son?"

"About a hundred and fifty."

Long stood up, looking at Son, smiling. "A stick a barrel. That's more'n you'd need to do the job. Let's see now, you got the two wires running out there under the ground. Insulated good, are they?"

"In some lead pipe," Son answered. He felt Aaron looking at him again, like he was crazy to admit anything. But Long was right and he was here. They couldn't get rid of him or shoot him for knowing.

"So every evening," Long said now, "you turn on your light. If it works you know your wiring's good and hasn't got corroded or chewed up by little animal creatures. Son, that's pretty good thinking. Though if you was to blow it, that would be a terrible way to treat good whiskey."

"I guess you can see the point of it though," Son said.

"Yes, sir, if you don't take the whiskey out yourself, nobody does. But things are different now, Son. You got a partner."

"How does that make it different?"

"You won't need to think about blowing up your whiskey. I mean *our* whiskey." Long stooped at the cupboard again. He took a spring knife from his pocket, reached in and cut the wire connected to the plunger. "So you won't blow up our business when I'm not looking," Long said. He lifted out the box, dropped it, and proceeded to smash it into pieces with the stock of his BAR. "Now then," he said, "let's figure out how we're going to run old Dr. Taulbee."

The only thing they decided for sure was that after dark Lowell Holbrook would slip out through the hollow and run home. If, Frank Long said, he wasn't afraid of being out in the

220

dark. Lowell said he wasn't afraid of the dark, that wasn't the reason he wanted to stay. But Son told him no, he had done a brave thing, but he wasn't going to stay here to get shot at; it wasn't his affair. Frank Long told Lowell he was the best bellboy he had ever seen and gave ten dollars for bringing his suitcase.

Son, with the 12-gauge, saw Lowell across the yard. Coming back, Son approached the barn from the blind side, slipped through the fence rails and got up close to the building and pressed his ear against a seam in the boards. He listened for about ten minutes before going in and feeling his way to the car. He waited again, briefly, before striking a match. There were blood stains on both the front and rear seats, but no sign of the three men. Son went out the back, the way they would have left, and looked out over the open pasture in the moonlight, at the brush shadows and the dark mass of trees beyond. Then he circled back, around the barn to the house.

Later in the night, listening, watching the slope, Son touched Long's shoulder and pointed out into the darkness. "Straight up there," he said. "You know where the grave would be?" Long said he thought he did. "Then put your gun on it," Son told him. "Right above it."

Son put his hand on the light switch. "You ready?" As Long answered, Son turned it on.

A hundred yards away on the hillside, the grave and the light post and a moving figure were illuminated and the BAR hammered

221

through the darkness until the figure disappeared and the light went off as Son flicked the switch.

"Buddy," Long said, "that's a good idea. It's too bad we can't pull it more than once."

"Maybe we can." Son was staring out at the darkness. One idea was leading to another, an idea that could end this; but he said no more to Frank Long.

fifteen

Friday morning, June 26, Dr. Taulbee made a decision: this would be the last day he could afford to sit out here in the piney woods, playing war.

It would be simple to outwait the man and starve him out. It had seemed simple before. But now, he realized, that could take a month for all anybody knew. Dr. Taulbee wasn't financing an extended campaign, or performing for the audience over on the ridge, or taking a chance that word of the siege wouldn't get in the county newspapers. That happened and before he knew it, the federal people would be driving up. No thank you.

He had been out here two days and two nights. To show for it he had four dead, another who probably wouldn't last the day, two more shot up, two cars out of commission, and eight men left who gave him sullen stares, waiting for him to think of something. He asked them, don't you want to get that boy's whiskey? Don't you want to get Frank Long? All right, a hundred-dollar bonus to the man that shoots him.

But he still had to convince them he knew what he was doing. He had to maintain their confidence. And, Jesus, if he didn't do another thing he had to keep them busy, away from the boy dying with the bullet in his chest. So this morning he kept six of them peppering away at the house with rifles while the other two drove to town to get Miley. He might as well keep Miley busy too. He had an idea for getting his boys in the mood for an all-out fight and needed Miley to help him.

The image Dr. Taulbee presented to the world that Friday morning was one of relaxed confidence. He sat in a wicker-back rocking chair on the porch of Son Martin's still, smoking a cigar, rocking gently, letting his tough boys from Louisville know he had the situation under control.

When Miley walked into the yard, looking around, frowning in the sunlight, she said, "What am I suppose to do out here? I can't shoot a gun and I never was a campfire girl."

Dr. Taulbee smiled at her and said, "As soon as you finish being a little sour-mouth smart-ass, I'll tell you."

Miley shrugged and waited, and Dr. Taulbee said, what she was going to do, she was going to march down the hill and tell Son Martin he had one last chance to give up and save his life.

And, if he acted at once on this offer, he would be paid a dollar a gallon for his whiskey.

Miley thought about it, picturing Son Martin. "And what do I do when he says no?"

"You come on back here."

"If you know what he's going to say, then what's the good of asking him?"

"Because of what you say when you get back."

"What is it I say?"

"In front of the men, you tell them all three of them down there are shot up and in pain, just barely dragging theirselves around with blood all over everything. They look to you like they won't last till night."

"Yeah," Miley said, "then what?"

"Then our brave boys, smelling easy victory, storm the house to finish them off."

Miley shook her head. "You sure are a thinker."

"You cute thing," Dr. Taulbee said, "give us a kiss before you go."

"They all out there again," Aaron said. "More than yesterday."

Son looked out across the pasture to the cars parked on the open ridge. "Come to see the show."

"I don't understand them people."

Son made no comment.

"Something else I don't understand," Aaron said. "Why you told him about the grave."

"He figured it out."

"He was guessing,"

"But he was right. Whether I said anything or not, he was right. If he gets out of this he'll dig for the whiskey and find it. But we can't shoot him because he knows where it is, can we?"

"I don't know," Aaron said. "Maybe *you* can't."

Son looked over at him, then at the ceiling. "There's something we can do if he stays up there long enough." He edged closer to Aaron at the window. "The light switch—"

"Hey, what're you two whispering about?" Frank Long's voice came from the hole drilled in the ceiling. Son's eyes raised. "We were just talking about you, Frank. Arguing which one of us is going to shoot you."

They heard him laugh. "Son, you wouldn't shoot an old buddy."

"You ain't an old buddy of Aaron's."

"What're you talking about?" Long said. "Hey, Aaron, I meant to tell you. I'm giving you a cut of the whiskey take, boy, so don't be having any dark thoughts. You hear?"

Looking up at the ceiling, Aaron didn't answer. He said to Son, "You want him with you?"

"No."

Son had made up his mind. He could say yes, thinking about the whiskey, the work and the years that had gone into it. He could say, all right, Frank Long is a partner. Finish this with his help. Maybe. Get the whiskey out and sell it with half the county knowing and watching and split the profit with a crooked federal agent he used to know in the Army. Do all that before another gang like Dr. Taulbee's heard about the whiskey and came down with their guns to start another war. Or before the Prohibition agents heard and started busting stills all over again. Forty-five hundred gallons of eight-year-old whiskey was a good idea at one time. Now it was a dream a man would have with his head under the covers, while he wished all the trouble it caused would go away.

He knew he wasn't going to drink forty-five hundred gallons himself and it didn't look like he was going to sell the whiskey. So if he didn't want anybody else to have it, there was only one thing left to do.

Blow it up. Splice the dynamite wire to the electrical system and turn on the switch.

If he could think of a way to keep Frank Long busy while he made the splice.

Walk up to him and knock him cold; that was one way. Hit him with a gun stock or a hunk of kindling if he had to. Then wire the charge and blow it and hope Dr. Taulbee would look at the smoke and go home.

That was the trouble. Son couldn't be sure what Dr. Taulbee would do. He was a scary son of a bitch, with his big smile. He might look at the smoke and go right out of his head.

Frank Long came downstairs with the BAR under his arm. "What I want to know," he said, "is who you expect will be coming next? Look-it out there."

Miley looked up from the porch steps to the house. "You got a ladder or is somebody going to pull me up?" She could see Son in the window. She didn't know Long was here until he opened the door and stepped out. When he leaned down to give her a hand, Miley continued to stare at him. Finally she let herself be pulled up. On the porch she brushed at the front of her skirt before looking at him again.

"It doesn't appear you're being held for ransom."

"I switched over, honey, seeing the error of my ways. That's a terrible person you're playing house with."

"He must have thrown you out," Miley said.

Long grinned at her. "How about yourself?"

"I've come with a message."

"Well, come in, honey; we want to hear it."

Miley looked around the room before her gaze settled on Son Martin. "You look all right to me," she said.

"We're getting along." Son realized he was glad to see her. He couldn't help smiling and she smiled back at him.

"Emmett says if you all want to quit now he'll pay you a dollar a gallon for the whiskey."

"We're asking five," Long said.

"*We* are." Miley raised her eyebrows. "We fit ourselves right in, don't we?"

"You want to be on our side?"

"It's a thought, isn't it?" Miley looked at Son. "I doubt if he can pay your price."

227

"Even if he could," Son said, "and was willing, the whiskey's not for sale. Tell him that. Not for a dollar, not for ten dollars."

"So you're still the one to talk to," Miley said.

"Tell him if he wants it he'll have to come get it."

"I expect he will. Though he's running out of people."

"How many we get?" Long asked her.

"Four, I think. Maybe five by now."

"Hey, Son, that ain't bad, is it?" Long looked at Miley again. "You sure you don't want to be on our side?"

"I'd have to think about it," Miley said. "It looks to me like the odds are still way against you."

"But changing all the time."

"That's true." Miley nodded. "But I still think he's going to win."

"I'll tell you what," Long said. "You stay here awhile with us and see how you like it."

"If I don't get back he'll send them looking for me."

"He might at that. What if we tell him we'll shoot you if he doesn't clear out?"

Miley laughed. "Are you kidding?"

"That's what I thought," Long said. "So we'll just keep you here and won't say anything and see what happens."

Son almost overruled him. He almost took Miley by the arm to push her outside; but he saw something—the way Long was openly looking at her body, peeling her clothes off with his gaze. Son went over to the stove. "You're going to stay," he said, "you might as well fix us some thing to eat."

Miley followed him over. "If that's what you want." Long's eyes were on the nice little can moving in the tight skirt. Son noticed that too.

"I'd like to see them run in there with the cars again," Bud Blackwell said. "Jesus, the one car went right through the barn."

"You hear that gun they got?" Virgil Worthman said.

"Like a machine gun." Bud pulled the weed stem from his mouth and made a noise like a machine gun firing.

Lowell Holbrook looked over at him. "It was a BAR rifle," he said, "belongs to Frank Long. Doesn't anybody know a BAR rifle when they hear one?" Gazing off at the house he walked away from them, like he wanted to study the house from a different angle. He knew the people were watching him.

Let them wonder what he was thinking. He had been in that house all yesterday afternoon until dark and he knew things nobody else knew. Last night and earlier this morning, nobody would leave him alone, all the questions they asked. Why had he gone down there? Wasn't he scared? How were they doing? Had any of them been shot? Lowell told them the man was a guest of the hotel; the man had wanted his car and his suitcase, so he delivered them. That's all there was to it.

Now, every once in a while, somebody would ask what he thought was going to happen. Lowell would study the house with his cool gaze and say, "Don't worry about Son Martin." A couple of times he wanted to add, "If you're so worried, why don't you go help him?" But he never did. If anybody wanted to help Son, but didn't do anything about it, it was their own personal business. A person knew what he should do and what he shouldn't do.

Lowell had a feeling for a while that Mrs. Lyons was going to do something. It had surprised him to see her drive up this morning. He would watch her when he remembered her being here. She stood by herself most of the time. Once she had asked him if he thought Son was all right and he gave her the answer, "Don't worry about Son Martin." She had looked awful worried; maybe it was true they were going to bed together. She had talked to other people, maybe trying to get them to help. But Lowell didn't see anybody getting any guns out of their cars. After a while Mrs. Lyons sat down on the corner of a blanket that a couple of ladies had spread. Lowell watched her holding a cup as one of the ladies poured coffee in it from a Thermos.

Everybody was sure prepared today. They had picnic baskets and coffee and Coca-Colas, blankets and folding chairs and canvas awnings built out from some of the cars. There was even a cookfire for anyone who wanted to fix a hot meal.

"Somebody ought to sell tickets," Lowell said

to Mrs. Lyons, and got a strange, sorrowful look from her, like she might be going to cry. Though she didn't.

The heavy-set guy, Carl, came over through the brush to tell Dr. Taulbee there was no sign of her yet, she was still in the house.

"They think they're pulling a stunt," Dr. Taulbee said. He blew a stream of cigar smoke toward the edge of the roof over the porch. "We start down there shooting and they tie her to the front door."

"If that was to happen, what do we do?" the man asked.

"You'd keep shooting."

"We been shooting, mister, for two days."

"Now when was it," Dr. Taulbee said, "somebody told me he was going to bring the nigger out dead and the other with his hands in the air? It seems to me it was the night before last. Well, buddy, I have been waiting for that to happen. I been watching you hotshots with your tommy guns and high-powered rifles, but I haven't seen any results. I don't know with all the shooting you been doing one of them is even nicked. Can you tell me that? If all this shooting for two days has hit anybody? No, you can't, buddy, because you haven't been close enough to that house to find out. Now tell me again how you're going to bring them out."

Carl's thick shoulders were hunched. He stood sullenly, looking up at Dr. Taulbee, who was rocking the chair slowly back and forth. "We'll get them out," the man said.

"Yes, I know you will," Dr. Taulbee said. "Sometime. Tell me something, is there any hay in that barn?"

"Plenty of hay."

"And there's a car in the barn?"

"That's right."

"If you were to get down to that barn just as it's getting dark—start the car up and get it loaded with nice dry hay."

"Yeah?" The man's sullen expression came alive then. "Set the hay afar and run the car into the house!"

"That'd bring them out, wouldn't it?"

"God*damn* if it wouldn't."

"Buddy," Dr. Taulbee said. "I think you got an idea."

"Miley," Frank Long said, stretching as he got up from the table, "You ain't much at the stove; but then a girl can't be an expert at everything, can she?"

Her eyes moved to Son at the window. "Some people like my coffee."

"Some hill boys will drink anything." Long grinned. "Hey, Son, I'm just kidding you. You got fine taste and good grub. I'll sit at your table any time."

Son looked over. "I'd appreciate you more at a window. You going back upstairs?"

"I guess I better."

"Well, see you later then."

Long reached for his BAR leaning against the table, then hesitated. "Hey, Miley, why don't you come up and keep me company?"

"I was going to do the dishes," she said, looking over at Son again.

"You can do them later. Son, you don't care if she does them later, do you?"

Crouching at the window, waiting for Long to get upstairs, Son shook his head. "I don't care."

"Honey, you can stretch out on the bed if you want, take a little rest."

"I'll bet," Miley said.

"What do you mean by that?" Long's tone was meant to sound offended.

"Oh come on," Miley said then, "get your gun and let's go up."

Watching the pasture and the hillside—and the light post far up on the slope marking the grave—Son listened to them mount the bare wooden stairs. He heard them in the room, the floor boards creaking. He heard Miley laugh. Long's voice came to them through the drilled hole in the floor. "Keep a close watch now, you hear?"

Son didn't raise his eyes. He said, "We hear," and waited in the silence of the room. He waited several minutes before glancing at Aaron who crawled over and put a hand on the Springfield, holding it on the window sill, as Son moved to the bullet-shattered opening in the wall and worked quickly with his knife, cutting the line to the light post and splicing the end of the dynamite line to the wire that

233

led from the switch down to the battery-powered electrical system. He covered the opening with the board Long had pulled loose, then removed it again. Long might notice the board and wonder why it had been put back. Son reached for a chair. He set it against the opening, then put his .38 on the chair with a box of cartridges, as if he placed the chair close to have the gun within reach.

Son leaned back against the grain sacks under the window. Looking up at the ceiling he lit a cigarette, wondering if Frank was having a good time, wondering how long he'd be up there.

When Miley came down, she put the coffee pot on the fire and asked Son if he'd like a cup. He nodded and watched her turn to the stove.

"You want to go back to Taulbee?"

He saw her shoulders move. "I guess so. I mean, where else is there to go?"

"What if something happens to him?"

"I don't know."

"Do you think about it?"

"Sometimes."

"What do you think you'd do?"

Miley turned toward him now. "I guess I'd look around, wait for an offer. Are you making one?"

"I was just asking."

"Do you want to go upstairs?"

Watching her, Son shook his head.

"Why, what's the difference between right now and the other day?"

"Do you see a difference?"

"I guess so. Or I wouldn't have said it like that."

"You want to shock me," Son said.

She nodded, slowly. "Do you know why?"

"I'm not sure."

"Because if you ever made an offer, no matter what it was, I'd probably take it. But you're never going to make an offer. There," Miley said, pausing, then turning to the stove again. "You can take that and do whatever you want with it."

Son got up from the window. "Pour me a cup," he said. "I'll be back directly."

Up in the bedroom, Long was sitting on the bed facing the window where the BAR leaned against the sill. He looked over as Son came in. "You want me to clear out?"

Son went to the window. He stood next to it looking up at the slope. "You remember last night," he said, "you got a shot at the guy by the grave?"

"I mentioned it was a good idea," Long said, "but would only work once."

Son looked at him. "What if I got Taulbee and the whole bunch to line up right there."

"How?"

"Tell them where the whiskey is."

"He wouldn't believe it."

"I'd go up there and start digging. They see the shaft entrance and the first barrels, they know it's true."

Long nodded. "While they're standing there I open up with Big Sweetheart."

"How's it sound?"

"You're standing there too, buddy."

"I wait till they're looking in the hole, then I make a run for it."

"Maybe."

"As I take off, you open up."

"I'd have to hit them the first time, wouldn't I? If they get to cover, you're dead."

"You hit that boy last night."

"I think I did."

"But you'd have to be sure I was out of the way."

"Come on, buddy, you think I'd fire while you was standing there?"

"I just mention it, Frank."

Long nodded, squinting as he looked at the later afternoon light filling the window. "It would be shooting the works, wouldn't it? If I don't hit them, they got the whiskey."

Son shrugged. "I don't see any other way."

"My, it's a chancy deal though, isn't it?"

"You want to try it?"

"How do we get the word to him?"

"Send Miley."

"I was just getting to know the girl."

"You don't have to shoot her."

"I was hoping not."

"She'd go out just a little way and call to them I'm coming."

"Well," Long said, "if you got the nerve, I got the gun."

Son frowned, making a face. "I hope I got

236

the nerve. Maybe I'd better think about it a little more."

"What'd you tell me about it for if you don't want do it?"

"I want to be sure, is all."

"Well, it's not something anybody can be *sure* of. Listen, we don't do it soon there won't be enough light. I want to be sure too."

"Let me study on it awhile."

"If you don't want to go up there," Long said, "I won't hold it against you, don't worry about that. But if you do want to go, we got to act quick. I mean it's your idea, buddy; it's up to you. I'll tell you what though. I think you can pull it off."

Son stared out the window, thoughtful. After a moment he said, "Why don't you go down and get some coffee. Let me think about it."

He remained at the window until the sun was behind the ridge and a shadow lay across the slope and darkened the sandstone wall above the grave. He waited until Long climbed the stairs again and stood in the doorway looking at him.

Son turned from the window, "I'm ready if you are."

"You want to do it?"

"I just made up my mind as you came up the stairs."

"Just a little too late," Long said.

"Why? It's still light out."

"Not over on the slope."

Son looked out the window. "You can see the post, the grave."

"But not clear; there ain't enough light."

Right now, Son told himself and looked over at Long again. "You know what you just said? Not enough light?"

Long was nodding, beginning to smile. "I was thinking the same thing. There's a light up there. All I got to do, as you start to run, is turn it on."

"You see any problems?"

"Not after that," Son answered.

He waited on the porch, leaning on a shovel, while Miley went out to the edge of the hardpack, where the path started across the pasture, and called out to Dr. Taulbee.

She would point to the house and yell out as loud as she could, "He's coming out! He wants to talk to you!" There was no response from the hillside, no sign of movement, but Taulbee must have heard. Miley's voice carried across the pasture, each word hanging sharply clear in the evening stillness.

Son looked over at the window, at the barrel of the BAR sticking out, at Frank Long and Aaron watching him. "I'll see you," he said, and jumped down from the porch and started off, the shovel pointing up his shoulder. Miley came toward him as she returned to the house.

"Take care of yourself, all right?"

"I'll be back," he said, not pausing, walking out to the pasture, his eyes on the trees and brush and the rock outcropping that towered above the grave, holding the slope in its shadow. He watched for signs of them, but saw no one until he was almost to the grave. Then a figure stood up among the rocks, a man pointing a rifle at him. Son kept walking until he reached the low fence around the grave and stepped over it. He saw several more men in the rocks now, but paid no attention to them. He began digging in front of the headstone. After a few minutes he could hear them coming toward him. Pushing the shovel into the earth with his foot, he looked up. Taulbee was coming out of the trees.

Son straightened now to wait, the handle of the shovel upright in front of him.

"I hope you're not pulling something," Dr. Taulbee said. "If you are, you're dead."

Son watched him come up almost to the fence. "I'm showing you where it is," he said, leaning in then throwing out another shovel of dirt. "I'm going to take your offer, a dollar a gallon, and clear out. Then it's up to you what you do with it."

Dr. Taulbee was in no hurry. He stared at Son, as if trying to see something else behind his words. "You're telling me the whiskey's buried here, in a grave?"

"It's no grave, it's a mine tunnel. You'll see." He began digging again, aware of Taulbee's men moving in closer. Taulbee placed one foot on the fence and leaned on his thigh as he watched.

"All of a sudden you just give up, uh?"

"I don't see any point in dying for whiskey."

"What does Frank say about it?"

"He doesn't have any say. It's my whiskey."

"You just suddenly change your mind."

"Do you want to listen to me talk or see me dig it up?"

"Go ahead," Dr. Taulbee said. "We're all anxiously awaiting."

After a few minutes the blade of the shovel struck something hard. Son cleared the dirt away and lifted out a board. "Look down in there," he said.

Dr. Taulbee leaned over the fence. "I don't see nothing."

"Get closer. Down in there you see part of the first barrel."

Taulbee stepped over the fence now to peer into the dark opening. "It might be a barrel. Take some more boards out."

"I'm giving you the whiskey," Son said. "I'm not going to dig it out for you. What you see is the end of a ditch that leads over there to the shaft entrance, where the slope gets steeper.

"I got to see more of it," Dr. Taulbee said, " 'fore I know for sure what you're selling me."

Son looked right at him. "You got a flashlight?"

"Over at the house."

Now Son's eyes raised to the post. "Well, there's a light right here we can use."

Taulbee looked up, squinting. "Turn it on." As Son stepped over the fence he said quickly, "Where you think you're going?"

Son half-turned. "To get the light put on."

"You can't work it here?"

240

"No, the switch's in the house. I got to holler for somebody to turn it on." Son started down the slope, feeling Taulbee and the men with the guns watching him.

"Hey," Taulbee called out. "That's far enough!"

Son stopped. "They won't hear me less I get a little closer." He started walking again, taking his time, moving steadily down the slope. When Taulbee called again, he kept walking, holding to the same pace.

"You hear me!" Taulbee yelled.

Son kept going.

"Another step, boy, we shoot!"

Son came to a halt facing the house across the pasture, a deserted-looking house, the two front windows dark squares in the shadow of the porch. He wanted to look around, to see how far he was from the grave. He could feel Taulbee and his men standing by the mound, all of them facing this way. Son didn't look back.

He called out, "Hey, Frank!" He was aware of the cars and the people on the ridge, way off to the right.

His eyes remained on the house. He was thinking, if you started running right now—there's a chance.

But then he said to himself, get your head out of the covers, boy. And he yelled, "Hey, Frank—turn on the light!"

There was a moment he would remember that stood alone, motionless, in dead silence. The moment ended and the hillside behind him exploded.

Frank Long's hand was still on the light switch as the sound rocked across the pasture and filled the hollows. As he looked out, the explosion shook the house and he saw the hill blown apart in a jarring string of eruptions that lifted smoke and earth into the air and billowed out to envelop the lone figure on the slope. As he watched, as the smoke thinned and rose against the sky, the first thing Long noticed was the outcropping of rock that crowned the heights of the ridge. Through the haze of dust he saw that the face of the wall was altered. Rock and brush had come sliding down in the explosion and now covered the upper part of the slope. There was no sign of the grave or Dr. Taulbee or his men.

The figure on the lower part of the slope was looking toward the rocks.

Long was outside before he noticed the people coming down from the ridge. A few remained by the cars, but most of them had started for the pasture, coming in straggling groups, coming almost hesitantly, but coming.

They stood looking past Son at the rubble covering the slope, at the place that had been a grassy hillside and the site of a grave. When he turned and walked down the grade toward them, they continued to gaze off beyond him

242

and above him, staring solemnly in the dust haze.

Bud Blackwell seemed about to speak, looking at Son for a moment, but said nothing.

Frank Long was the only one who spoke. He said, "After all that work, uh?"

Son didn't answer. He was aware of Long and the others as he walked past them toward the house. Without looking at anyone directly, he was aware of familiar faces, the Blackwells, the Worthmans, and Stampers; Lowell Holbrook standing awkwardly; Miley Mitchell, alone, watching him; Aaron on the porch, holding onto a post, waiting for him. He wondered if Kay was here, though he didn't look for her among the solemn faces.

Son walked on until he was almost to the yard. It was here that he stopped and looked back and said, "I got a half barrel and some fruit jars if anybody feels the need."